THE CADAVER

A Selection of Recent Titles by Guy N Smith

BLACKOUT *
NIGHT OF THE CRABS
THE SLIME BEAST
SNAKES
THE SUCKING PIT
WEREWOLF BY MIDNIGHT

* *available from Severn House*

THE CADAVER

Guy N. Smith

This first world edition published in Great Britain 2007 by
SEVERN HOUSE PUBLISHERS LTD of
9–15 High Street, Sutton, Surrey SM1 1DF.
This first world edition published in the USA 2008 by
SEVERN HOUSE PUBLISHERS INC of
595 Madison Avenue, New York, N.Y. 10022.

British Library Cataloguing in Publication Data

Smith, Guy N.
The cadaver
1. Children - Wales - Death - Fiction 2. Horror tales
I. Title
823.9'14[F]

ISBN-13: 978-0-7278-6570-0 (cased)

Except where actual historical events and characters are being described for the storyline of this novel, all situations in this publication are fictitious and any resemblance to living persons is purely coincidental.

All Severn House titles are printed o

Typeset by Palimpsest Book Pro
Grangemouth, Stirlingshire, Sco
Printed and bound in Great Brita
MPG Books Ltd., Bodmin, Corn

For Diane Bird – a special friend

He cast upon them the fierceness of his anger, wrath and indignation, and trouble by sending evil angels among them. He made a way to his anger; he spared not their soul from death.

Psalms 78: 49–50

Part One
Before Death

One

The group of children huddled against the grey stone wall on the street corner were almost invisible in the thick fog, which had been seeping down from the mountains throughout the afternoon. With the onset of an early dusk, the street lighting struggled to penetrate the deepening gloom.

It was just possible to make out the clock face on the tower at the bottom of the hill where the Narrows met with the steeply sloping main street. A landmark, it had overlooked this small Welsh border Parish for a century like a Cleopatra's Needle, watched generations come and go, hurried their passing with its quarterly chimes.

It struck four times, the noise eerily muffled by the fog.

A teenager in the furtive gathering started and peered nervously about him. He licked his dry lips, pursed them. He had already thought up a reason not to be here, was trying to muster up the courage to voice it. If you ducked out of anything which the Morgan boys had planned, they could make life decidedly unpleasant for you. Like the time Scrumpy Smith had chickened out of a raid on the Reverend Crawford's orchard in the vicarage garden. Next day Scrumpy's bike tyres were slashed. Everybody knew who had done it but nobody made any accusations, in case Rick or Tom Morgan got to hear.

Further down the street the small store was crowded, kids on their way home from school buying witch and vampire masks, maybe a bottle of fake blood to add a touch of reality; the produce store down at the bottom of the hill had long sold out of pumpkins. Fiery faces would bob in the foggy darkness later on tonight.

Trick or treat.

'It's too early yet.' Mickey Farrell finally found the courage to voice a quavering protest. 'We oughta meet up later.'

'You gettin' windy, Mickey?' The others did not have to see the sneer on Rick Morgan's face to know that it was there. His gangly frame belied its strength as he eased himself away from the wall, his every movement menacing. He might have been taken for sixteen instead of twelve; the licencees of the pubs used that excuse to allow him to play the machines; if they refused then there was always the chance of a window being smashed in the night. Or worse.

His hand toyed with a knife in the pocket of his cammos. He always carried a knife. For fishing. Nobody could dispute the fact that he fished, mostly when he played hooky, and one didn't go down to the river bank without a knife.

'*No*!' The denial came out in a rush, the swallow was audible even against the background of slow moving traffic.

'Good.' Rick laughed, an unpleasant sound. 'We don't want nobody gettin' windy, do we, Tom?'

'No.' Tom Morgan always agreed with his elder brother, he had long learned not to disagree. This was why he had fifteen police charges against him, mostly for petty theft. Often he shouldered the blame for Rick's crimes. The cops didn't hurt you; Rick most certainly would.

''Course we don't.' Rick eyed his companions, his gaze moving slowly, threateningly, from one to another. ''Cause we're gonna be *cruel* to *Kroll*!'

The worn-out joke was greeted with hollow, forced mirth. Bodies shifted uneasily, everybody was staring at the house opposite, as fearful of it as they were of their leader.

The three-storeyed terraced dwelling was built of the same grey stone as the rest of the houses in the Narrows, quarried from up on Panpunton hill four centuries ago. This one looked no different from the rest, the swirling grey vapour hid its shabbiness, the rotting window sills, a length of guttering that had pulled away from the wall. But the watchers knew it only too well, they passed it every day on their way to and from school, and each time their mouths went dry and icy shivers ran up their spines and prickled the hairs on their necks. They tried not to look, hurried on past, but it made no difference.

They shuddered now and it had nothing whatsoever to do with the raw October evening. It was as if Death had reached out and touched them, reminding them that one day he would call for each one of them. Maybe sooner rather than later. Perhaps tonight if they stayed around here too long.

'Look's like he's out.' Mickey's tone lacked conviction.

'Na, he never goes out at night.'

'Or maybe he's died.'

This time there was no laughter. Death was something you didn't joke about. Not now, anyway.

'He's in there, all right.' It was as though Rick Morgan had to muster his own confidence this time, called upon the others to support him, seeking approval over what he had in mind. There was safety in numbers. Maybe. 'He's gotta be, he can't be nowhere else. There's only one way we're gonna find out.'

They cringed visibly, drew back into the shadows.

'He might call the cops, Rick.' It was one of the others who spoke this time, not Mickey Farrell.

'So bloody what?' A shaft of misty orange street light revealed the arrogance on Rick Morgan's features. 'What can the cops do, I ask you? Is trick-or-treating against the law?'

Their silence confirmed what he already knew, that they were shit-scared of the old man, more frightened of Edward Kroll than they were of him. And that made Rick very angry.

'Scared of a crazy old fucker, eh?'

'He gives me the creeps.' Tom Morgan answered for the rest of them. 'He's like a . . . a walking corpse.'

'The walking dead, huh?' The leer was gone, those furtive eyes were fixed on the house opposite. 'Yeah, I guess you're right, Tom.'

Everybody followed Rick's stare. Windows, behind which no lights showed, dead eyes that saw and guessed why you were here. A door with peeling paintwork, warped by the damp mountain atmosphere. It might have been shut for ever.

A tomb of the living dead.

'Aw, he's probably at the back, in the kitchen.' Rick needed to reassure his companions or else they might just walk away, go home.

'He ain't,' Mickey Farrell spoke up, braver this time, ''cause I came that way, up from the Cwm. There ain't a light showing in the whole house.'

'He's taken to his bed, then. A cold or bad flu.' Or died. The thought came unsolicited, griped Rick's stomach. 'We'll fetch the fucker out. You got them apples, Mickey?'

A plastic carrier rustled, glinting yellow in the dark; it weighed heavy in the hand that held it aloft. Apples from the vicarage orchard, not stolen but those that had fallen on to the street side of the high stone wall, lain rotting amidst the mulch of autumn leaves in the gutter. Mickey and Brendan Hughes had retrieved them with gloved hands because of the drowsy wasps that still clung to the decomposing fruit.

They had laughed about it in yesterday's bright sunlight, there didn't seem any harm in it then, just a Halloween prank. All that had changed now.

'Light the lantern, then, because we have to make it look like we're only doing it for Halloween.' Rick had thrown an egg at Kroll's door last week, by daylight. Maybe the dried yolk stains were still there, it was impossible to see in this light. Hit-and-run. Run for your life.

Tom Morgan rattled a matchbox, Mickey held the gouged out pumpkin, steadied it with his free hand. A match flared, extinguished.

'Fuck!'

'The bloody wind!'

'There's no wind, Tom, not a breath.'

Tom's skin prickled, he looked across at the house again. He was no scholar but suddenly, for no accountable reason, lines from a poem he had read for his English exam came unprompted into his mind.

No head from the leaf-fringed sill
Leaned over and looked into his grey eyes,
Where he stood perplexed and still.
But only a host of phantom listeners
That dwelt in the lone house then
Stood listening in the quiet of the moonlight
To that voice from the world of men.

Tom Morgan almost screamed, any other time he would not have remembered a line of Walter de la Mare's *The Listeners*. He didn't want to, he hated anything associated with learning.

Was that curtain moving as if somebody was hidden behind it, watching the street below? It was probably his imagination, it was playing tricks tonight.

'Shield it for 'im, Tom. Christ, don't say I've got to light the bloody thing for you!' Rick yelled, and had them all glancing at the house.

And he felt in his heart their strangeness,
Their stillness answering his cry.

'I'll be OK.' Tom got the match to burn this time and, with shaking finger, pushed it through the jagged mouth hole and found the candle wick inside. The squash face lit up, the eyes flickered, seeming to glance furtively in the direction of Kroll's house. There was no mistaking the expression of fiery fear.

It was all a trick of the candlelight.

'Ready?' The fog had thickened considerably these last few minutes; Rick's question sounded muffled, went unanswered.

'Go knock the door, Brendan.'

A half-step forward that checked, threatened to retreat.

'Go on. Hurry!'

There was no hurry, just that every one of them wanted to get it over and done with, to be away from here and back in the safety of their own homes where lights burned brightly and there was nothing to be afraid of. They would have left this minute had it not been for Rick Morgan. His word was law, even beyond the school precincts.

'Knock that fucking door!'

They all watched as Brendan crossed the narrow street. Apart from themselves, the town was suddenly deserted, the store was empty, other shops appeared to have closed early. The pavements no longer echoed with hurrying footfalls; wherever folk had been going, they had arrived, safe and snug. Just the Halloween pranksters remained, rooted by a terror that transcended their fear of Rick Morgan.

In the toyshop window a cut-out witch, suspended by an almost invisible wire, bobbed up and down on her broomstick, a grinning caricature that mocked them. It had lain in a dusty store room for a whole year eagerly awaiting this night. An inanimate portrayal of evil that tonight scented evil.

Go knock that door.

Timid knuckles rapped on solid woodwork, a drumming that seemed to intensify, magnified of its own volition within the silent, darkened recesses of the house; a tattoo that slowly died away to let the silence surge softly back.

Brendan backed off, almost losing his balance on the kerb, then scurried back to the comparative safety offered by his companions. The shadows retreated, dodging the wavering glow from the pumpkin lantern, fog eddied down the street.

'You got them apples ready, Mickey?'

Mickey Farrell's grip squelched a cold, wasp-eaten Bramley. Throw it and be done, splat the door and run like hell. Like Rick's egg, all the old man would find would be a stain.

Run whilst there's still time.

There's nobody home. The thought process of anticipated relief; an unanswered knock, a bag of rotten apples tipped back into the gutter whence they had come. It almost happened. But not quite.

No head looked over from a leaf-fringed sill. A bird flew up from under the eaves where it had been roosting. The watchers stood listening in a fogbound night stirred and shaken by their intrusion. The last truck had rumbled on past the clock tower below, the town was silent and deserted.

The cardboard silhouette witch had slowed, watching and waiting, because this was her long-awaited night. Evil was abroad in many forms; some visible, others unseen.

'*Somebody's coming!*'

It was almost a cry of terror. It could have been Rick who called. Or Tom. Or Brendan. Or Mickey Farrell. Or all of them or none of them.

The door was opening, the fearful onlookers sensed it long before they heard the steady creaking of unoiled hinges. Another gust of icy air almost blew out the candle in that fear-filled pumpkin. Instead, it fanned the flame, cast its wan glow on that doorway across the street.

The clustered watchers screamed mutely at the sight of Edward Kroll.

He clutched at the doorpost as though, without its support, his hundred-pound frame would have crumpled to the floor. Sunken eyes glared out of blackened sockets, fixed their audience with a hateful stare. Nostrils flared as if he scented the night air, the lips were compressed into a thin, bloodless line so that at first glance the face might have been deemed mouthless.

But it was the manner in which his skin was taut and stretched like age-old parchment that had the onlookers cowering; the hollowed cheeks gave a skeletal appearance.

An out-dated rumpled suit hung from the wasted frame, a scarecrow in a field, hastily erected so that it sagged and stooped, a trilby hat jammed down on the head as an afterthought.

A corpse. A cadaver resurrected in a suit of clothes.

'Fling that fuckin' apple, Mickey!' Rick's command was a cry of terror, a parting shot before the retreat began. His companions were huddled, faces turned away, impeding one another in their panic.

Mickey Farrell threw the apple for a number of reasons: it was cold and squashy in his hand and he needed to get rid of it; he had an inbred fear of wasps and there might be one in the fruit he clutched; a kind of bravado before he fled. But mostly because Rick Morgan had ordered him to throw it and he dared not disobey.

It was a kind of compromise, a lob rather than a throw. He could see Kroll squinting out into the darkened street, mouth pouted in irritation, annoyed by the disturbance, this intrustion on his privacy.

Mickey Farrell had a clear sight of his target.

The home-made lantern hissed, it was scared, too.

Run!

The apple hit Kroll full in the face, burst. The impact had him staggering back so that he almost fell into the hallway behind him. He pawed at the stinking morass with bony fingers, made a noise like he was blowing his nose, spitting, retching. The faded wallpaper on either side of him was mottled brown as he shook his sticky fingers.

His arms windmilled with a rage that was only just beginning.

'*Stupid boys*!' A shriek, he stumbled out on to the pavement as though in pursuit of his tormentors.

'Trick-or-treat?' a voice shouted out.

A howl of anguish answered, a finger shook accusingly, threateningly. His neck stretched as if he sought to identify those who had dared to do this to him, but all that was visible was a fiery, grinning countenance. A tongue of flame protruded cheekily, was extinguished; shadowy shapes hustled one another as they ran. Apples that had spilled out of an abandoned carrier bag bumped and rolled down the sloping driveway.

Edward Kroll stood there on the pavement wiping his face with a grubby handkerchief; dabbing, squeezing juice from the saturated material, anxious in case it had stained his suit.

Finally, he went back indoors, closed the door behind him, muttering incoherently to himself. It was the Farrell boy who was responsible for this, he had recognized him briefly in the light from the lantern, the very same boy who, last summer, had thrown a stone through one of the front windows.

Mickey Farrell would pay dearly for the act which he had perpetrated this night, Kroll vowed.

The witch in the shop window found her momentum again, began to rock to and fro, grinned her delight. Her long wait had not been in vain, this most precious of nights was truly alive with unspeakable evil.

Two

There was a choice of three eating houses in town, apart from the coffeehouse which only served cookies and snacks on toast to a regular clientele of ladies who met there to discuss matters appertaining to the upper social circles. The Clocktower Teashop concentrated on a healthier menu, baked potatoes and microwaved meals. Ginger's and the Grillhouse vied for the custom of those seeking a more satisfying meal, home-made steak and kidney pie or a roast of the day.

Edward Kroll, in all the years he had lived in Knighton, only ever patronized the Grillhouse, possibly because it was in close proximity to his dilapidated home. He always dined there on Tuesdays and Thursdays, arriving punctually at one forty and departing at three ten. His timing was as precise as the mechanism of the clock on the tower just down the street, which was as irritating to the proprietors, John and Christine Morgan, as it was to their customers. Mostly, though, the regulars timed their eating habits in order to avoid sharing the small restaurant with the recluse.

'He smells,' Aggie, the ageing school cleaner who met her friend, Barbara, there for a quick coffee every morning at eleven, announced in a loud voice through a cloud of cigarette smoke. 'Not BO, mind you, he's always clean enough in himself, washes and the rest, but 'ave you ever seen 'im wearing anything else except that brown suit, Barb?'

'Can't say I have,' Barbara replied as she accepted a light from her friend and inhaled deeply. 'You're right, Ag, it's that suit that stinks, never been cleaned, I'll warrant.'

'Or changed!' Aggie gave a bronchial cough. 'Meself, I reckon the bugger sleeps in it!'

'Beats me what 'e does with 'imself, shut away in that bleedin' house all day long.'

'Reads them books of 'is.' Aggie shook her head in disapproval. 'That's what 'e does.'

'And 'ow the hell do you know, Ag? Been to visit 'im, 'ave you?'

'Not me!' Aggie exaggerated her horror at the very suggestion. 'I wouldn't set foot inside for a week's wages and a Christmas bonus! I'll tell you 'ow I know.' She lowered her voice to a hoarse whisper. 'Me nephew, Dai, you know, Betty's boy, 'e's an electrician, and a few months back 'e 'ad to go and do a job there. Sommat technical, I can't remember what it was, it doesn't matter, anyhow. Well, Dai says the place gave him the creeps as much as Kroll 'imself did. The bugger stood there watchin' 'im all the time, wouldn't let 'im out of 'is sight. Didn't say nothin', just watched, scared 'e might pinch somethin'. Dai says 'e'd never go there again. The house was full of books, every bloody room. Not on shelves like any normal book-readin' person might have 'em, but stacked all over the place and thick with dust. And *toys,* too!'

'Toys!'

'That's right.' Aggie gave way to another fit of coughing, drew hard on her cigarette. 'You know, dinky cars and lead soldiers like me brother used to 'ave when we was kids. And stamp albums. You name it, Kroll's got it hoarded in there, re-livin' 'is childhood, but mostly books. Dai said there was piles of comics, too.'

'Harmless enough, I suppose,' Barbara said as she drained her cup and looked at the clock on the wall.

'In moderation, I say. But if you shut yourself away with all them kind of things, it's got to 'ave an effect on you, 'asn't it? Look what it's done to 'im, for Christ's sake. It's no wonder the schoolkids plague 'im. Tell you sommat else . . .' Aggie glanced around to make sure that the room was empty. She heard the clink of crockery, muffled voices from the adjoining kitchen; the Morgans were busy preparing for the lunchtime regulars. 'Them Morgan boys 'ave been at it again.'

'That don't surprise me.'

'There's a story goin' round the school that they knocked Kroll's door and pelted 'im with rotten apples when 'e answered it. What they call Trick or treat. Except that they made young Mickey Farrell chuck the apples, and they've made sure everybody knows, just in case Kroll calls the police. Bad 'uns they are, them boys, they'll end up in jail as soon as they're old enough, you mark my words. They couldn't 'ave better parents but young Rick and Tom go wild once they're outa sight. All the kids are scared of 'em at school.'

'I'll have to be going.' Barbara stubbed out her cigarette, scraping her chair back, and spoke in a voice loud enough to be overheard in the kitchen. 'The Grillhouse is a credit to Knighton, Ag, best meal in town and the tourists pack in here in the summer.' Barbara wanted to disassociate herself from Aggie's comments about Rick and Tom just in case the Morgans had been eavesdropping.

Christine Morgan had overheard. She had been busily preparing their most popular snack dish of the day, Yorkshire pudding in a bowl with a choice of fillings, when Aggie's resonant whisper had reached the kitchen. Christine's first reaction was anger; anger because that damned woman was a gossip, spread innumerable stories, whether they were true or false. Then fury over what her sons had done; she did not doubt the authenticity of the school cleaner's report of last night's happening. A mother's intuition told Christine that Rick and Tom had been up to something the moment they walked into the house. She just prayed that it was nothing too bad, nothing which would result in another visit to the police station, maybe just a caution or a charge. Well, it could have been a lot worse. And it had been Mickey Farrell who had thrown at Edward Kroll, the boy was the real culprit for being stupid enough to do what others told him. She always tried to find an excuse for her offsprings.

'What's up, Chrissie?' John Morgan came back into the kitchen, tying on a clean white apron; the jaunty angle of his peaked chef's cap knocked a year or two off his thirty-five. The heavy moustache suited him, Christine had finally decided, even if it was greying prematurely ahead of his dark hair. He had put on a few pounds around his waistline, that was due to nibbling whilst he helped her prepare food, as well as his recent lack of exercise. Formerly a school sports instructor, the change to restaurateur was somewhat drastic. She must try to get him to take more exercise.

'Nothing.' She turned away so that he could not see her expression. Auburn haired and slim, she had taught home economics at a private school; she had never thought that one day she would put her theory into practice, sell meals instead of instructing pupils how to cook them. Life could have been almost idyllic in this remote border town except for Rick and Tom. Their misbehaviour was responsible for the lines that were beginning to etch her attractive features.

'Yes, there is!' He caught her arm, pulled her round to face him. 'Look, darling, we've always shared our worries and the only ones we've got are those sons of ours. What've they been up to now?'

'All right . . .' She fought back her tears. 'Nothing much, I suppose, compared with petty theft and vandalism. I overheard Aggie telling Barbara that Rick and Tom made Mickey Farrell chuck rotten apples at old Kroll last night.'

'Maybe they'll earn themselves a medal apiece for it', John said with a grin. 'I thought for a minute they'd done something serious. Boys will be boys, as they say.'

'Unless Kroll goes to the police.'

'Mickey threw the apples, he didn't have to. Anyway, I've come close myself, on more than one occasion, to tipping a bowl of apple crumble over his head. Trouble is, it wouldn't have much effect, he never takes his bloody hat off, even when he sits at the table. He's been coming in twice a week for the five years since we took this place on and I couldn't tell you whether he's got a head of hair or whether he's as bald as a coot. Which reminds me, today's Tuesday.'

'I hadn't forgotten.' She put a tray of Yorkshire puddings

in the oven to keep warm. 'Which means there'll be an early rush, all the regulars eaten and gone by half twelve. Ugh, that man is the nastiest, most revolting person, I've ever known.'

'Still, it's regular money in the winter when there aren't any tourists about,' John said as he began scrubbing some carrots, 'and in the summer visitors are birds of passage, here today and gone tomorrow. If they decide not to eat here again, it doesn't matter because next day they'll have moved on to the coast. Passing trade, you take their money and wait for the next ones.'

'I can't even bear to look at him through the serving hatch.' Christine grimaced. 'It takes him an hour and a half to eat his meal, he cuts his meat into minute pieces, chews each one to a mulch and dribbles gravy down his chin. And in between mouthfuls he's muttering away to himself. And if you happen to go through, he talks to you. About books mostly, and I've never been a book person.'

'I had a laugh the other week . . .' John seized upon an opportunity to make light of his wife's depressed mood. 'Kroll was having his lunch and in walks Daisy, and you couldn't have anybody dafter than her. She orders a tea and a bacon sandwich and goes and sits with *him*! He didn't much care for that, tried to ignore her but she kept rattling on about how she was sixty-seven and still looking for a man. Suddenly, there's this loud fart and I thought to myself, Gawd, Daisy's gone and blown off. Then I heard that laugh of hers and her saying, "Don't mind me, Mr, it's better out than in!".'

'I don't think it's funny at all!' Christine walked to the sink and swilled her hands under the tap. 'I can tolerate crazy folks like Daisy but Kroll's vulgar and nasty with it. He *frightens* me, John.' She paled, her fingers shook visibly. 'He's *evil*!'

'I think that's going a bit far.' John was taken aback by his wife's reaction. All the same, he, too, felt uneasy about Kroll, more so these last few weeks. It was as if he was somehow changing, in a way that the restaurant owner found inexplicable.

* * *

At exactly one forty the bell on the outer door clanged. John Morgan tensed, anticipated the loud bang with which the door was shut, the shuffling footsteps across to the table in the corner; followed by the incoherent mutterings as Edward Kroll debated with himself on whether to choose from the snack meals on the menu, the 'specials' on the blackboard, or perhaps to try the 'chef's dish of the day'. Today it was chicken supreme. But, having weighed up every eating possibility at length, Kroll would order the all-day breakfast. Because it was Tuesday. On Thursdays he had cottage pie with apple crumble to follow and a cup of tea. Tea, definitely not coffee, he would insist with an aggressive vehemence, because coffee kept him awake.

Nothing changed and it was not likely to today.

'Good morning, Mr Kroll', John went through into the dining area, an affable approach was second nature to him these days. No matter how much folks ruffled you, you put on an air of affability, got rid of your frustrations later. 'Not a nice morning, this fog doesn't look like lifting today.'

Kroll looked up, he muttered something that was inaudible. Then: 'I don't get up very early in winter. Bed is the warmest place, it doesn't cost anything to heat and I can get away with just using the central heating for an hour or two. I keep my overcoat on the rest of the time. It also makes an ideal eiderdown spread out on the bed.'

John noticed the slight aroma of staleness, of unwashed clothes. It all figured. 'Of course, I'd never thought of that.'

'Take a tip from me, then.' A low, humourless laugh. 'Now, after much deliberation over your exquisite menu, I think I'll settle for the all-day breakfast. With two eggs, please, lightly done, and an extra slice of toast, the bacon done to a crispness but not burned.' A white, emaciated hand came up from his lap, a grubby Tupperware sandwich box was laid on the table alongside his side plate. As usual.

'Thank you, Mr Kroll. John turned back to the kitchen, heard his customer get up from the table, shuffle across the carpeted floor. An habitual use of the toilet before eating.

The bolt clicked, John Morgan heard the tap in the wash-basin running, envisaged a lathering of bony hands, a vigorous drying on the roller towel. A muttered 'clean hands, clean dick', then came the flushing of the lavatory. A kind of ritual, the Man's own peculiar code of cleanliness being enforced.

'Done just the way you like it, Mr Kroll,' John said as he placed a steaming plate in front of the man.

'Excellent.' Kroll might not have eaten for a week by the way he grabbed up his knife and fork. Then, with meticulous deliberation, he cut the slice of bacon in half. The sections of fried tomato were segregated, the meal was divided into two equal halves, because, as was customary, half the contents of his plate would be carefully placed in the container, to be heated up for supper back in the dismal confines of his cold, damp dwelling.

John paused in the entrance to the kitchen. He didn't have to watch, he didn't want to but it was a kind of compulsion, maybe to satisfy his own curiosity that nothing had altered, a confirmation of the 'Kroll stories' that had long become a worn-out repertoire amongst the other diners at the Grillhouse.

Kroll reminded John of the hamster they used to keep when Rick and Tom were young, chewing vigorously with pouted mouth, ravenous yet seeming to make little impression upon the food placed in front him. Kroll would wipe his plate clean with the last morsel of toast at precisely two thirty-five, leaving not so much as a grease stain, masticating his last mouthful as appreciatively as the first.

'*Pudding*!' A shrill bellow, a clattering of cutlery on crockery. Rude and infuriating, the only antidote was to grin and go through with a bowl of apple crumble and custard. One became an unwilling actor in the other's crazy scenario. All because one had to earn a living in winter when trade was restricted to regular custom.

A cup of strong tea was demanded at two fifty, before the dessert was finished. A mahogany brew which had stewed in the pot on the Rayburn in readiness. They kept a special cup for Kroll, removed the stains with bleach.

Kroll took a loud slurp, grimaced. 'The best that I can expect outside my own home, I suppose.' His lips stretched in the closest he ever came to a sardonic smile. 'There is only one way to make a *real* cup of tea.' He set the cup back in the sacuer. 'Proper tea, not teabags, but if you only buy bags, and I can't imagine why, then split the sachet open and pour the whole of the contents into the cup or mug. Then, add a little boiling water and allow the brew to mash for at least five minutes before topping up. Three spoonfuls of sugar, then just a dash of milk. The powdered variety is better, after all milk is only a whitener, isn't it? Of course, it is.' He seemed agitated, excited because he was expounding a theory that was all his own.

'We always try to make your tea as you like it, Mr Kroll.'

'You don't have to drink it all at one sitting,' Kroll continued, appearing not to have heard. 'The luxury of a microwave enables one to heat the beverage up when it cools.'

John glanced at the clock. Three p.m. As predictable as he had been over the years, Kroll fumbled a pack of cigarettes from his pocket.

'I always smoke Red Band . . .' He paused to draw from the flickering flame of the match held with unsteady fingers, and puffed out a cloud of smoke. 'They're the best value for money and the cheapest in the shops. I collect the fronts of the packets, I've got them banded into dozens.'

John Morgan sensed an icy trickle at the base of his spine. This guy was crazy. Like Chrissie said, he gave you the creeps. It had not bothered John till now. He detected a smell that definitely did not come from stale clothing. He stepped back a pace, tried not to make it obvious. A faint noise like a balloon slowly deflating in the area of the chair upon which his customer sat. He backed off a little further.

'How much do I owe you, Mr Morgan?' Kroll pinched out the tip of his cigarette, stowed it carefully away in his breast pocket; he rationed his tobacco habit, smoked a cigarette in three sessions, as he had explained on a previous occasion. This one he would enjoy again later, possibly after the supper which he had saved in the Tupperware box.

'Three pounds, twenty-five pence, if you please.'

Kroll started, visibly jerked upright in his seat, almost spilling a jangle of coins from the leather purse which he was in the act of opening. 'Three pounds, twenty-five! The same meal last Tuesday cost me three pounds, fifteen! There must be some mistake.'

'No.' John pointed to the menu, and became aware how his hand was shaking. 'If you note, prices rose as from today, November the first.'

'What!' A sudden childish petulance, the open clasp was snapped shut, the purse waved in the air. 'I had no notification of a price rise. This is preposterous, inexcusable, way beyond the rate of inflation.'

'I'm sorry.' Jesus, I don't have to apologize but I can't help it, John said to himself. 'Food prices have risen. Eggs and bacon have gone up, so have mushrooms and other vegetables. I've kept prices down as long as possible. Maybe Ginger's . . .'

'I have never been inside that place and, furthermore, I have no intention of doing so. Have you not thought of giving regular diners a discount?'

'We really can't afford—'

'I'll pay you three pounds, twenty pence, and the same every Tuesday, not a penny more!'

'Oh, all right, I'll make a concession in your case.' You bloody creep, you've let him browbeat you with his meanness, he's got a lunch and a supper cut-price. Some kind of powerful, inexplicable force seemed to emanate from this weakling in a shabby suit and a trilby hat; John found himself yielding to it. A personality that was not strong, just nasty. Christine's words came back to him, echoed in his brain. *He's evil*!

Nine minutes past three: Edward Kroll was shuffling towards the door, pausing to check his reflection in the window, adjusting his hat by it.

'Good day, Mr Kroll.'

Kroll stopped, turned slowly, and John Morgan found himself recoiling from the other's expression. The skin seemed to have stretched even further over the cheekbones and forehead, the eyes had sunk deep into their cavernous sockets. Surely a ten-pence price rise could not have fanned such fury as seethed within this frail body.

'Mr Morgan . . .' The words were a reptilian hiss, bad breath fanned John's face. 'Your disreputable sons paid me a visit yesterday evening.'

'Oh! I'm sure they didn't, you must be mistaken, Mr Kroll', John's lower lip quivered.

'I am not mistaken.' The voice was barely audible and all the more terrible for that. 'They and others. They were not the sole culprits although I suspect that they instigated the stupidity. A rotten apple was thrown . . .' Kroll's head was thrust forward so that his wrinkled and sinewy neck stretched out of the frayed grey scarf that was wrapped around it. 'It hit me in the face.'

'I . . . I apologize on their behalf, my wife and I will certainly speak to them about it.'

'That is up to you, I have no quarrel with either yourself or your wife. My quarrel is with the boy who made this assault upon my person. He will be dealt with in due course.'

'I sympathize with you, Mr Kroll, it is not a pleasant experience to . . .'

Edward Kroll was peering at the clock on the wall, straining his sunken eyes, his lips twitching with irritation. He had overstayed by two minutes and he was a man of inflexible punctuality.

'I merely warn you, Mr Morgan. Whilst there is still time!'

And then the man who was Edward Kroll was gone, a pathetic hunched figure shuffling away into the fog that shrouded the town, his corpse-like features hidden in the folds of his scarf.

Three

'What you bin up to, Mickey?' Linda Farrell half turned from the sizzling chip pan as the door opened, surveying her son with exaggerated disapproval. At thirty, she was grossly overweight and had abandoned all attempts to retrieve her once presentable figure. Her slovenliness was apparent in her soiled clothing and straggly hair. There came a time in life, she had told Ellen next door only yesterday, when you accepted your lot and lived for today.

'Nowhere,' he answered sullenly. If it wasn't 'nowhere' it was 'somewhere', he had two alternatives for an evasive reply when he was guilty of some misdemeanour.

'It's half past five, you should've been home at four, especially in this weather. The fog's so thick you can't see across the road. Now, where've you bin till now? And I want the truth.'

'Trick or treatin'.' Mickey dropped his school bag on the floor, and would have dashed for the stairs except for his mother's 'Oi, just a minute!'

'What?'

'Never mind "what", just look at yourself in the mirror. Go on, take a look, see for yourself.'

Mickey looked in the stained and grimed mirror that hung at an angle on the side of the crockery cupboard. He saw his own overweight body but he had long ceased to notice that. It was his expression, his pallid complexion, the fear in his wide eyes that shocked him. Even the dirty glass could not disguise that.

'You're tremblin' Mickey, shakin' like a leaf. Come on, what've you done? You'd better tell me. You've been off up to no good with the Morgan boys, and don't deny it!'

She turned back to the basket of spitting fries, lifted it clear of the pan and shook it.

'We've only been Trick or treatin'. Honest.'

'Early for Trick or treatin', ain't it? Most of the kids on the estate don't go out until after dinner.'

'We went early. 'Cause of the fog.'

Linda could usually tell when her son was speaking the truth. Tonight she thought there was a vestige of truth in his reply; maybe a quarter truth and three quarters lies.

'With the Morgans?'

'Yes.' He looked down at his mud-splattered shoes, fidgeted with his fingers.

'What's that mess all over your hands?'

He opened out his fingers, stared at the sticky brown mulch that slimed all over them. 'Apples, I guess.'

'Apples! You've bin in the vicar's orchard, then?'

'No, I swear it. We picked up some that had fallen off the trees overhanging the road, that's all.'

'What for? They're rotten at this time of year.'

'For Trick or treatin', that's what. I *told* you!'

Her eyes narrowed. 'You've bin throwin' apples, 'aven't you? Knockin' on doors, and when somebody answers, you pelt 'em, just as the kids on the estate 'ave been doin' all week, which is why we've 'ad the cops ridin' round every day. I guess you're goin' to be in trouble, Mickey.'

'No, it wasn't me, I swear it, Mom. Not *all* week. We just went to the one house.'

'*Whose*?'

'Kroll's. You know, the old geezer who lives up in the Narrows . . .'

'*Jesus wept*!' Linda Farrell looked heavenwards, lifting the chips clear of the spitting fat. 'You won't half be in trouble. Kroll will phone the police for sure. Ugh, that guy gives me the creeps and the nearest I've ever been to 'im is across the street! I've heard what others say about him, though, and that's enough for me. A bloody ghoul, and I'd prefer you to keep well away from 'im in future, but it seems like you've gone and done it now!'

'What's wrong with 'im, Mom?'

'He's a bitter, twisted dirty old man, that's what. And as mad as they come. 'E's bin livin' in that house as long as ever I can remember. They oughta put 'im away, keep 'im in a home. If he recognized you . . .'

'He couldn't've done, it was dark and foggy.'

'Let's 'ope 'e didn't, then, for your sake, but you can bet that if 'e did, then the police'll be round 'ere and you'll be down at the station bein' charged by PC Morris, like you was that time you threw a brick and broke the streetlamp top of the estate.'

'The Morgans *made* me do it, Mom.' Mickey was close to tears.

'Well, you don't 'ave to do what they say.'

'They'll beat me up if I don't.'

'And if they do, it'll be the police cautioning them because *I'll* tell the cops. Bullies and vandals those lads are, as well as bloody thieves, and comin' from a posh 'ome, too. It beats me. Now, get your food, your dad's gone to the pub already, bloody lives there 'e does! And you're not going out again tonight, you've caused enough trouble as it is.'

'Aw, Mom, it's Halloween!' Somehow the protest was no more than half-hearted, a token one. Secretly, Mickey had no wish to go out into the foggy, fear-filled night again.

'You've already done as much trick or treating as you're going to do this year,' she stated as she began piling chips on to a couple of plates. 'An early night for you tonight, and no playing truant tomorrow. Understand? And if you 'ave any more trouble from those Morgan boys, you're to tell me.'

For once, that night Mickey Farrell went up to bed early. The incident had left its mark upon him, fear rather than guilt. Not fear of the bullying Morgans but of an old man who skulked in a damp, dark house and who had, by his own reclusion, become the nemesis of the townspeople.

Sometime during the night hours Mickey dreamed that he was back in the Narrows as he tossed restlessly in a pile of rumpled bedsheets. He was all alone, there was no sign of the others, and the fog was thicker than he had ever known it. The street lamps struggled to filter an eerie orange glow, houses and shops were in total darkness and no traffic trundled through the town.

Everybody had left town because of Kroll, Mickey had been abandoned here. A movement in the murky shadows attracted his attention, a glimpse of a silhouette, familiar in a long coat and brimmed hat, was all he needed to bring a scream to his lips.

Edward Kroll prowled the deserted streets, a hunting beast of the darkness that had scented its prey and shuffled in pursuit.

Mickey ran but the Narrows was too steep for his unfit, overweight body. A daily diet of fries with everything that went with them, and sometimes did not, was not conducive to an athletic build. His feet felt like they wore concrete shoes, his chest was heaving as he fought for breath. He was no match for his shuffling, snuffling pursuer. A skeletal, icy cold hand reached out, rose the hairs on the nape of his neck.

'Please, Mr Kroll, I didn't want to throw that apple, Rick Morgan made me. He'd've beaten me up if I hadn't.'

Kroll accepted no excuses, he wasn't interested in hearing them. His wasted features seemed to glow luminously in the foggy dark, his eyes were embers that had burned their way deep into his skull. His bloodless lips moved, pouted, muttered. Mickey could not hear what the other was saying but he understood just the same.

You threw the apple, Mickey. You're going to pay for your foolishness with your life.

No!

Mickey woke up shaking, and such was his terror that he switched on the light and left it burning until his mother came in at quarter-to-eight the next morning to wake him up for school.

'You don't look good, Mickey.' Linda Farrell wore a shabby housecoat, her hair was tangled and matted, her eyes were black-ringed. 'You bin poorly in the night?'

'I was sick,' Mickey lied.

'It's no wonder, you gettin' up to them sort of tricks. I expect you've got yourself all knotted up worrying whether or not Mr Kroll's goin' to call the cops.'

Mickey nodded, he would not confess to his nightmare. If he worked this right there was a chance of a day off school without playing hooky. 'I've hardly slept at all.'

'In which case there's no point in me making you go,' she sighed. 'Your dad won't be going to work, neither, 'e 'ad too much to drink last night. Well, you'd better stay home, but mind –' she wagged a finger at him – 'no going out to play. In fact, you'd better stop in bed this morning and catch up on some sleep. And if you're feelin' better later, then you can come downstairs and watch the telly. Don't go playin' your radio 'cause your dad's tryin' to get some sleep, too, and you know what 'e's like if 'e gets disturbed!'

Mickey knew only too well. After his mother went out of the room, he lay back in bed and stared at the window. The fog seemed even denser than last night, the street lighting was still struggling to penetrate it. It was going to be one of those dark days today when it never seemed to get light.

Mickey dozed, drifting off into a dreamless sleep. It was late afternoon when he awoke and a glance outside showed him that it was dusk again. The fog was typical of this mountainous region, once it came down, it sometimes lasted for days. It might go on for a whole week.

All too soon it was bedtime again.

The fog still had not lifted by the following morning; in a way it was like a continuation of Halloween. Mickey shuddered at the memory. All the same, he had to go to school today, there was no way that his mother would tolerate him staying home for two days.

He joined up with a crowd of other kids along the estate, all walking to school. He experienced a feeling of safety in numbers. They did not appear even to notice his presence, it was one of those depressing mornings that did not encourage conversation. There was not so much as a malicious joke made about Mickey's obesity and that in itself was a relief.

He knew that they would cross the road and go down

Market Street – it was the shortest route to school. As they approached the junction, Mickey lagged behind, hung back: Market Street joined the Narrows where Edward Kroll lived.

None of the others seemed to be aware that Mickey was no longer with them. He stood there on the kerbside, watching the dense grey vapour devour them. Then, just as he had been in his dream, he was all alone, except for the continual stream of slow-moving traffic.

The longer route was the lesser of the two evils as far as Mickey was concerned. Much as he hated any form of physical exercise, he dared not pass Kroll's place with its dead-eye windows watching him. He set off, dragging his feet, scuffing loose gravel. His calves ached, his breath clouded in the damp, cold air. This morning his lungs were wheezing, he might even be starting a cold. If he was, then that guaranteed him another few days off school. Safe from the Morgans.

Safe from Kroll.

He was breathless by the time he reached the top of the steep main street by the clocktower. Shopkeepers were opening up for business, an ironmonger in a grey smock was stacking cans of kerosene in his passage entrance. Cars and vans crawled, bumper to bumper, their headlights cutting swathes through the grey vapour.

The clock on the tower began to chime, resonant dongs. Nine o'clock.

You're late for school. Mickey Farrell. The words jarred his brain, a muttered warning. He stiffened. It was as though Edward Kroll had spoken to him from out of the enshrouding fog.

The Green Cross Code: Mrs Jones impressed it upon her pupils at school. Look right, look left, look right again. Then, if the road is clear, cross.

A half glance to his right, he quickly jerked his head away, in case he chanced to look up the Narrows and saw . . .

It would be impossible to see anybody in the Narrows, even the tower was barely visible from here. But in his dream Mickey had seen Kroll in the fog *and* the dark. He shied from the prospect.

Look left; the traffic was at a standstill down at the bottom of the hill, obstructed by a brewery wagon unloading at the Knighton Hotel. That was fine for Mickey.

Look right again. *No way*, he couldn't.

That was when Mickey Farrell gave way to a fit of panic. He dared not look right; he had to cross the road.

It was as though somebody beckoned him from the far pavement, signalled to him that it was OK to cross because the traffic was momentarily halted. Likewise, it seemed that some invisible force pushed him gently from behind.

Go on, Mickey, what are you waiting for? Cross now. Run!

Mickey dashed into the road, called upon every flagging reserve in his desperation to reach the opposite side. His shaking legs tried to drag him back, some instinct yelled at him not to go, but he ignored it. Passers-by turned their heads, horrified expressions on their faces; a woman started to scream.

Mickey heard a screeching of brakes, tyres squealing. He closed his eyes and then came a brief moment of excruciating pain just before everything blacked out.

Four

A rural police officer's life is mostly routine but never boring. The varied duties might range from a spate of sheep rustling to investigating a case of juvenile vandalism in a nearby town. Occasionally a road accident, seldom a tragedy.

Hardened as he was to violent death, Mickey Farrell's accident had shaken PC Phil Morris. One accepted adult fatalities, child deaths were distressing. Even more so when one knew the family concerned and you were faced with the unpleasant task of having to break the news to the parents.

Phil had spent most of that fateful foggy morning attempting to console Linda Farrell. In the end, Dr King, a legend in his own lifetime and now nearing retirement, had sedated her. Her husband, who either showed extreme courage, or was not particularly bothered by their son's death, took her to stay with her parents.

The boy had been troublesome but had never committed a serious offence; lazy certainly, he played truant on average once a week, he had been caught shoplifting in the gift shop last year. Just sweets, he had been let off with a warning. His main problem had been that he was easily influenced by others. Like the Morgan boys and one of these days – Phil eagerly anticipated it – they would get their just desserts. In the meantime, the tragedy overshadowed everything else.

The constable had had a note on his pad to pay a visit to the Farrell household that day, anyway. He had scheduled it for his last call of the day before going off duty, it would be preferable to talk to Mickey in front of his parents after school and then let it go with a warning to the boy not to throw rotten fruit, or anything else for that matter, at members of the public. It was just a Halloween prank that had gone too far but the fact remained that a complaint had been made and it had to be followed up.

All that was of no consequence now. Except that, according to the rule book, the complainant must be notified of the outcome. And Phil Morris did not relish the task of calling upon Edward Kroll.

The policeman could maybe, justifiably, have let the matter rest in view of the circumstances. Mickey's funeral had taken place today, it seemed that the entire population of the town had turned out to pay their last respects. St Edward's church had been packed to the rafters and those unable to find a seat inside had thronged in the doorway, down through the lychgate and out into the road. Here they joined in the singing of the twenty-third psalm and 'Abide With Me'.

Kroll had not been amongst the mourners; Phil had not expected him to be. The old bastard was maybe sitting at home, rubbing his wasted hands and gloating because the boy had got his just desserts. But that was, possibly, judging Edward Kroll unfairly. He never attended any gathering, only emerged from his refuge for his twice-weekly repast at the Grillhouse or to make a few meagre purchases from the shops. A police officer had to be impartial, emotions must never enter into a case.

PC Phil Morris's motive for calling upon Kroll was purely a selfish one, no matter how he attempted to convince himself otherwise. There was always the possibility that the vindictive old man might write to the chief inspector at the area station in Llandrindod Wells to the effect that his complaint had not been executed because a police officer had not called on him to report on the outcome.

Kroll might not even be aware that Mickey Farrell was dead, that was a distinct possibility. All that was required of Phil was to inform the other that the boy had been killed in a tragic road accident and, sadly, that was an end to the complaint.

As he walked up the Narrows, Phil sensed the grief that hung over the town, just like the week-old fog that had thinned but not dispersed. People went about their business as usual but few paused to converse as was the habit in small communities; heads nodded, token muttered greetings were exchanged. The Clocktower Teashop was deserted, whereas most mornings mothers on their way home from delivering their young children to school gathered to gossip over cups of coffee. The whole town was gutted by the bereavement as surely as if it was one of their own kin who had died beneath the wheels of a delivery van.

Phil rounded a bend, saw Kroll's house up ahead of him; it was distinctive by its shabbiness, had the appearance of a deserted building. Something else he noted that sent a little shiver up his spine: passers-by crossed the road, walked on the opposite side, as if they feared to pass too close to the place. Which was ridiculous, the officer thought, if it wasn't his imagination, it was probably because of Kroll's dripping downpipe, or because there was more room on the other side.

Phil glimpsed an expression on a woman's face, half hidden by the woollen scarf wrapped around her head; a quick sideways glance in the direction of Kroll's abode, as if to reassure herself that he was not watching from one of the grimed windows, her eyes jerked away as if she was frightened to look.

Kids on their way home from school suddenly ran, slowed once they were past the lair of their nemesis; they did not glance back, hurried on their way. A teenager, delivering evening newspapers, skirted that front door with its peeling paintwork. In all probability the occupant was too mean to purchase a copy, yet there was something decidedly disturbing about the way townsfolk shunned that place, as if they lived in dread of Edward Kroll.

Phil approached the door, knocked on it, stood back and waited. More people hurried past him because they did not wish to linger in the shadow of Edward Kroll's dwelling place. He began to feel uneasy, too, and tried to shrug it off. Because he was a policeman; he represented the law and Edward Kroll was not above the law.

Phil's trained ears strained in the hope of picking up a sound from within; an approaching footfall, a movement. Anything.

There was nothing, just an awful silence that seeped out from beneath the ill-fitting door.

Perhaps Edward Kroll was not at home, he had ventured out on some errand. No, he was not in any of the shops, Phil had glanced inside every one on his way up the street, in the manner that an officer of the law did. Just checking, keeping shopkeepers on their toes, just in case one of them might have been tempted to sell cigarettes or liquor to an under-age customer. That way you kept the respect of the traders without appearing to enforce the letter of the law, a police presence was often an adequate reminder.

Kroll would not be in the Grillhouse because it was Wednesday and too late in the day, anyway. He could only be in one place. At home.

Phil Morris knocked a second time. He could have gone away, recorded the fact that he had called at the complainant's house but there was no answer to his knock. His conscience refused to let him leave, it would be tantamount to cowardice, pandering to the fears of the townspeople, fleeing from Kroll. It would also be a neglect of his duty, a senior citizen's non-appearance could not be ignored, it would be nothing short of negligence. Kroll might have suffered a stroke or a heart attack, might be lying unconscious on the floor.

Or dead.

Kroll's years were indeterminable but he was surely way beyond middle age. Perhaps sixty, or nearer seventy. His emaciation made it almost impossible even to guess. If there was no answer to a third knocking then Phil would have to find a means of entry, force one if necessary.

Even as the disturbing thought entered his mind, Phil heard faint shuffling footfalls on the other side of the door. A key grated in the lock, a bolt was forced back with no small amount of effort, accompanied by the sound of laboured breathing at the sheer physical effort required.

The door scraped open just enough for Edward Kroll to peer out from beneath the brim of his greasy felt hat.

'Can I be of assistance, officer?'

The words were harsh, almost a hiss, a reprimand. The expression was one of annoyance at being disturbed.

Phil started, recoiled. During the course of his police career he had viewed corpses in varying stages of decomposition, some that had lain undetected for a week or more. It had been his duty to answer the calls of those who had not seen an elderly neighbour lately, to investigate. This was far worse but it was still a call of duty. He took a deep breath, got himself back under control.

'May I have a word with you, sir?' Maybe he could have told the other everything he needed to know standing out here on the street. Professionally, one went indoors, talked in confidence. And Phil Morris was a professional.

Kroll hesitated, there was suspicion in those deep-sunken orbs. His tongue flicked out like a gila monster, he gave a hollow cough and saliva dribbled down his chin.

'About the hooligans?' He spat the question out. The dribble string swung like a pendulum. Another deep rumbling cough.

'Yes.'

'Come inside, please.' Kroll strained his frail body, the door was dragged back.

A stench wafted out from within, an aroma of staleness that came out in a rush as if it had lurked in the unlit passageway awaiting this opportunity. A cloying smell that rasped the back of the policeman's throat, a coldness that was colder than the damp atmosphere outside. He shivered.

'Thank you, Mr Kroll.' The officer squeezed inside, instinctively shying from brushing against the puppet-like figure that clung on to the open door for support. He heard Kroll forcing the door shut, and momentarily experienced a trapped feeling.

Abandon hope, all ye who enter here. Now that was just plain bloody stupid, he was angry with himself. He was an officer of the law and, as such, he must act with dignity and command respect.

'Go on through to the end room. It's warmest in the kitchen.'

Anywhere had to be warmer than this freezing corridor, its space restricted by cardboard boxes that were stacked neatly but precariously against one wall, their contents labelled in spidery, barely legible, handwriting. Books were stacked in piles on top of them, threatening to avalanche at the slightest vibration. The door at the far end was ajar, a shaft of light from an unshaded bulb slanting through.

The small kitchen was obviously Edward Kroll's living quarters. Phil stared in disbelief. The single window, had its glass been clean, would have looked out on to a narrow yard; a high ceiling, shelves from floor level reached right up to it, books and magazines stacked as tightly as the space permitted. A cooker that was either broken or not used, because it was thick with dust. In contrast, a microwave was positioned on the hob.

The table was covered with a greasy oilcloth, loaded with convenience provisions. Clearly, the occupant only used one plate and ate out of packets and containers: a McVitie's chocolate cake had its wrapper neatly folded back to where it had last been sliced; biscuits, plain and chocolate stood in their packets: corned beef that was half-eaten from its can. A cup of dark brown tea had gone cold, having formed a scum on the surface.

The officer's stomach churned, he felt nauseous.

'Would you like a cup of tea, officer?'

'Er . . . no, thank you, all the same.'

'Please excuse me whilst I re-heat mine. I drink sparingly, often a cup lasts me most of the afternoon.' Kroll lifted the cup, it was as though its weight was too heavy for him, he slopped some of the mahogany coloured liquid as he transferred it to the microwave. The effort brought on another spasm of coughing.

'You don't seem well, sir.'

'A slight chill, nothing more!' The reply was abrupt. 'This fog doesn't agree with me, I try to remain indoors except when it is absolutely necessary for me to go out.' A bell clinked. 'Ah, that should be about right now.'

Kroll slurped noisily, smacked his thin lips in appreciation.

'About the apple throwing incident, sir.'

'Ah, yes!' The other's eyes blazed instant hate as he set the cup down in a space on the cluttered table.

Phil noticed a line of jars of jam set out like a row of toy soldiers on parade, labels all facing in the same direction. In front of them were a similar array of coins, piled in their respective denominations. Doubtless Kroll had counted them, knew the value of each tiny stack, the total amount. He probably had it recorded in a notebook somewhere, deducted what he had spent after each foray into the outer world. The guy was sick, he should be in a hospital.

'Doubtless, you are aware of the tragedy that has struck this town, Mr Kroll?'

'Tragedy? No, I'm afraid I don't involve myself in local gossip and the only newspapers I read are national ones. Mr Morgan, the proprietor of the Grillhouse, gives me a copy of the *Mirror* on my visits. The previous day's issue, of course. Nevertheless, it enables me to keep up with current affairs. I—'

'Mickey Farrell is dead, Mr Kroll. Killed by a vehicle.'

'Oh, I see.' The lips stretched, there was no mistaking the satisfaction in the leer. 'Then there is little point in pursuing my complaint, is there? I trust, officer, that you spoke to the boy before the accident happened?'

'No, I didn't!' Phil almost shouted, his fists bunched, his knuckles whitened.

'Justice has been done in the extreme,' the cracked voice announced with undisguised gloating. 'One really can't muster any sympathy for today's delinquents, officer. Vandalism and assault are roads to hell.'

'Mickey Farrell was just an ordinary kid, there was no real harm in him.'

'He was evil, like those Morgan boys. I have already spoken to their father about their loutish behaviour and I trust that he will administer suitable retribution. The decline in standards in our society is due to two causes, the absence of suitable deterrents and an undisciplined upbringing of their offspring by parents. I—'

'No crime was committed, a Halloween escapade went too far.'

'I was hit by an apple, a rotten one. That constitutes assault, officer, as you will find out if you consult your superiors!'

'But no real harm was done, it is insignificant compared with the events that followed.'

Kroll did not hear him, a fit of coughing which had been gathering force in his lungs bent him double. Spittle sprayed over the table, a string of phlegm dangled from his contorted lips. His frail body shook as he clutched at a chair.

'You're ill, sir!' This time it was the policeman who gloated. You've got lung cancer and you'll die a slow, lingering death. And this town will rejoice, there won't be a single person who will mourn.

'I am *not* ill!' Kroll straightened up, he was retching but somehow he got it under control. 'A slight chill due to this inclement weather but if I stay indoors, in the warm, it will go. Now, as it seems that further action regarding my complaint is impossible, I must bid you good day, officer. However, I must reiterate my comments regarding other young troublemakers in this town and request you to be extra vigilant. Should I have cause, I will telephone the station and I shall expect my complaint to be dealt with swiftly. Do I make myself clear?'

'*Every* complaint is dealt with, sir, as speedily as possible!' Phil Morris turned away as he fought against an urge to run down the passageway, drag the front door open and flee out into the street.

'So it seems.' Edward Kroll's voice was a low, mocking whisper. 'Justice is swift and harsh, however much the law tries to protect miscreants. The guilty do not go unpunished.'

Five

Edward Kroll had always been a messy and fastidious eater but never more so than on this drizzly Thursday which preceded Bonfire Night.

From the doorway through to the kitchen, John Morgan furtively observed his only customer with no small amount of disgust. Particles of chewed meat from the cottage pie adorned the edge of Kroll's plate, even this array of rejected food was aligned systematically.

Ugh! The proprietor of the Grillhouse did not want to watch this meticulous mastication but, for some inexplicable reason, it had become a masochistic compulsion. The revolting consumption of an already cold meal had become a subject of fascination. In a way, it was hypnotic.

It was sometime before the realization dawned upon John that Kroll was unwell. He shivered even though the radiators in the room were fully turned up; John had even considered opening one of the windows because the atmosphere was stifling and the panes were opaque with condensation. But, even when in good health by his own standards, Kroll protested vehemently at the intrusion of fresh air. Any customer who unwittingly failed to close the door upon entering was reminded of the omission with a screech of admonishment.

Today Kroll was quite clearly cold. The brim of his hat was pulled down firmly over his forehead as if to protect him from a biting north-easterly gale, and his scrawny neck was swathed in his old scarf. His topcoat was fully buttoned and, whilst he chewed, he rubbed his thin hands together vigorously.

Half the contents of his plate, divided into exact equal portions, were already inside the sandwich box; the remnants, smaller than the special 'children's choice' meal, seemed scarcely to have been touched.

He's ill, John decided, probably got a bout of flu, there are already several cases in town. Dr King had forecast an epidemic by Christmas, had mentioned to John and Christine that immunization jabs were available if they wanted them. They would probably take the doc up on his offer later in the week; when you ran a restaurant you could not afford to be ill.

Kroll's influenza might turn to pneumonia in the cold dampness of his house; John felt guilty at the thought, it was like he was wishing it on the other. Kroll had stopped eating altogether now, just sat with his head in his hands, his meal discarded.

'Mr Kroll, are you all right?' John came through into the dining area and approached the lone customer. The last thing he wanted was for Kroll to collapse here. Jesus, I don't want to have to touch the old bastard! Another nauseating thought, suppose he needed the kiss of life! John Morgan almost threw up.

Kroll's dulled eyes peered out from between splayed, near fleshless, fingers. He began to cough, the phlegm in his lungs gathered momentum.

'A slight chill, nothing more.' He regained control of his speech. 'I think I shall dispense with the pudding today. If you have a suitable container I can borrow, I'll take the apple crumble home with me. And I'll drink an extra cup of tea on my next visit. After all, both are included in the price of the set meal.' A handful of coins had been laid out on the table in readiness, neatly arranged in descending order of value.

'I'm sure the wife will find an empty ice-cream container or something similar.' John failed to keep his contempt out of his tone but Edward Kroll did not appear to notice. John reached out for the finished plate.

'No, no. *No*!' A sudden explosion of anger at the presumption that the remains of his meal would be scraped into the waste bin. 'I abhor waste, Mr Morgan.' With some difficulty Kroll prised the lid off the Tupperware box. The plate seemed almost too heavy for him to lift; he scraped with his knife, deposited the remnants of his cottage pie into a morass on top of that which he had already saved. 'There! Waste not, want not. Thank you, Mr Morgan –' his voice sunk to a throaty whisper – 'and if your wife will be kind enough to box the dessert for me, I think I shall make an early departure today. Home beckons.'

'I'll fix your pudding.' Bile scorched the back of John's throat as there was another decidedly unpleasant smell coming from the area which Kroll occupied.

'Oh, and by the way . . .' Kroll's compressed lips were virtually invisible.

'Yes?'

'Have you spoken with your erring sons yet about their appalling behaviour the other night?'

John tensed, his eyes closed for a second. 'No, actually I haven't . . .'

'*Why not*?' Aggression showed in a skeletal mask.

'Because . . .' John instinctively stepped back a pace, a ball of chewed meat slid off the tilted plate, splatted on to the carpet. 'Because . . .' *Oh, Jesus Alive!* 'Other things have taken precedence over it.'

'Like what?' The scarf-wrapped neck jutted forward.

'Mickey Farrell's death. His funeral. Rick and Tom are very upset.'

'So they should be! Doubtless they were the cause of that boy's death, not that I have any sympathy for him! Most likely he was playing a stupid infantile game of chicken, trying to dodge between the traffic, on their instigation!'

'He was *not*!' John Morgan yelled. 'He was alone, no other boys were with him, there were witnesses. There was a thick fog . . .' He gave a sob. 'And I take umbrage at your insinuations, Mr Kroll.'

'Please yourself.' Kroll waved a deprecating hand. 'I think it serves as a warning to other members of our young decadent society, don't you? One's sins are returned with interest, ultimately the guilty will be punished, some sooner than others. Please remind your sons of that, Mr Morgan. Before it is too late for them also!'

* * *

'How dare he!' Christine was sobbing with rage in the kitchen. 'You shouldn't have let him have his pudding, John. He certainly wouldn't have got it if I'd known at the time what he said. It's outrageous! You should have deducted the cost of what he didn't have and told him never to come here again. He's a disgusting old man. *I wish he was dead*!'

They were both trembling; with anger foremost, but underlying it was fear. Fear of Edward Kroll. Fear of death. It was as if Kroll had put a fatwa on the younger generation of Knighton.

'He may well die, from pneumonia, judging by the way he's shivering and coughing. Anyway, we can do with every customer we can get during the winter months.' John Morgan was ashamed of his cowardice. There was a lot he should have told Kroll but he hadn't because, like everybody else in this town, he was afraid of the recluse.

'We'd doubtless get a few more customers if *he* stopped away,' she said as she clinked plates angrily as she dried them. 'I've never wished anybody any harm before but . . .'

Christine left the sentence unfinished, dried her hands on a towel. 'I'd better go upstairs and check on Rick and Tom. I've never known them stay home before during half-term week, makes me wonder if *they're* sickening for something, too. And don't you dare tell them what Kroll said.'

She almost ran for the stairs, Edward Kroll's threat had made her uneasy.

It was a relief to find Rick and Tom in the upstairs lounge. The PlayStation was switched on but they weren't playing with it, they just sat there on the sofa with the controls in their hands, just staring at the screen.

'Are you OK, boys?' Her relief turned to unease. They didn't sit around normally, or, if they did, it was usually to play computer games and to quarrel over them.

'OK.' The reply lacked conviction.

'No, you're not.' She moved in front of them, scrutinized them. Their features were pale, their eyes black-ringed as if they had not slept last night. Heads bowed because they did not want to meet her gaze. 'There's something wrong or else you wouldn't be sitting here like this. Come on, I want to know what it is. What've you been up to now?'

'Nothin', honest.' Rick looked at Tom, glanced away again. 'Is *he* still here?'

'Who? Your father?'

'Na. Kroll.'

'Oh!' Christine tensed. 'So it's him that's worrying you, is it? Well, you needn't worry, he left about ten minutes ago and if I have my way, he won't be coming back here. According to your father, Kroll is ill, but I doubt it'll be anything serious.'

'I wish he'd die,' Tom muttered.

'That's not nice,' Christine admonished as she remembered her own wish of a short time ago and felt guilty. 'However bad anybody is, you must never wish them dead. Edward Kroll isn't bad, he's just nasty.'

'He's . . . *evil*.'

Christine bit back a retort, she had no wish to scare her sons. Kroll must be played down, portrayed as just a despicable old man, nothing more. 'Come on, that's a bit over the top. Now, why don't you go outside for a while, just a short walk? Go across to the newsagent and fetch me an evening paper and I'll give you the money to go to the gift shop and hire a film for this evening. How's that for a fair bargain?'

They looked at each other, shook their heads. 'We don't want a film, Mum. We don't wanna go out, either.'

There was no mistaking the fear in their eyes, it was as though they were skulking upstairs in fear of their lives.

'You're afraid to go out. She spoke softly, her words were barely audible. 'Is it in case you might meet Kroll?'

A subdued 'yes' answered her.

'Well, there's no chance of that,' Christine said trying to sound cheerful, 'because he never goes out except when he comes here to eat on Tuesdays and Thursdays. Anyway, as I told you, he's ill so he's probably in his dirty old bed right now. You don't even have to pass his house to fetch a paper and a film. So, what's keeping you? I told you, Kroll won't be going out so he can't possibly hurt you.'

'He doesn't have to go out to hurt you, Mum,' Tom muttered, he was close to tears.

'That's nonsense, how can he possibly hurt you when he's inside that dingy old house of his?'

'He wasn't out the morning . . . the morning Mickey got killed.' Rick seemed to cower on the sofa, glancing around as if he feared that their nemesis might be crouched in a corner of the room.

'What's that got to do with it?' Christine sensed her flesh beginning to goosepimple, her stomach had contracted.

'Kroll doesn't have to go outside to get you.' Tom's voice quavered. 'He can do it from home. You ask anybody in town, and not just kids, they'll tell you.'

'This is utter nonsense.' She had suddenly gone very cold.

'No, it isn't.' Rick was suddenly panicking, yelling at her. 'You don't understand, Mum. *Kroll killed Mickey Farrell*!'

Six

Dr Mervyn King's dapper, iron-grey moustache bespoke military service at some time during his life, a reminder of far-off days in India and Afghanistan when the British army maintained peace around the globe. At one stage in his career he had served with the Gurkhas.

He was due to retire the following summer; he had heard whispers of a party planned in his honour at the community centre. The prospect was more daunting than the time when he had been awarded the Military Cross for bravery in the heat of battle. His abrupt manner concealed a kindness that embarrassed him, his brusqueness was a front for his shyness. There were many stories concerning him which spanned the three decades during which he had been in town, most of them true.

He could have been excused for taking life a little easier, letting his two younger partners share the night shift between them and attend to the daily home calls which amounted to a considerable mileage each week in this scattered community.

But it was not his nature to ease off; if anything, he was working harder now than he had done at any time in his life. 'A doctor is never off duty' he reminded his long-suffering wife when he answered an emergency call out in the middle of the night. Each patient was treated as an individual, he made time to listen to them, no matter how crowded the waiting room was during surgery hours.

Today he was faced with a dilemma, and indecision was not one of Dr King's shortcomings. In the privacy of his book-lined study, in his large half-timbered house adjacent to the recently built health centre, he permitted himself a rare pipe of tobacco. Smoking was unfashionable, anti-social, these days; he wasn't hypocritical, merely diplomatic. Pipes were less harmful than cigarettes but the distinction was a grey area within the medical profession. It was preferable for a doctor to be considered a non-smoker rather than to deceive one's patients deliberately. After all, even a doctor was entitled to one small vice.

King debated with himself whether or not to contrive a call on Edward Kroll. He had checked that the man was registered as a patient but, annoyingly, his record card had disappeared from the files. It had probably got lost in the move here from the original surgery. It didn't really matter, not at this stage anyway.

Mervyn King had bought this practice in the 1960s. He tried to remember if Kroll had lived in town in those days; nobody really seemed certain when he had taken up residence in the Narrows. The house had been empty for years, probably since the war. Generations died off without passing on such trivial information to their offspring.

There were rumours, of course; embellished supposition. The original owner had died, the house had remained unoccupied for years, allowed to fall into a state of disrepair. Kroll had bought it as a retirement home but because of his reclusive nature it had been a long time before anybody realized that somebody was living there. In effect, Edward Kroll had just appeared.

Now, apparently, the man was ill. Seriously. PC Morris had mentioned it to King, the constable considered it was his duty to inform the doctor. Likewise, King felt that it was his responsibility to check on Kroll.

One couldn't force a patient to have treatment, it was a delicate situation. The doctor was under no obligation to investigate a second-hand report, most would have shrugged their shoulders; if a guy wanted to die, that was his business. But Mervyn King was under an obligation to his own conscience.

At least he should make some attempt to see this man, Kroll; if he refused to be examined or treated, then Mervyn could rest easy in the knowledge that he had done his best. He was honest enough with himself to admit that curiosity played a part in his proposed home call; there was gossip around the town, he had overheard snatches of it in the surgery waiting room.

Kroll killed the Farrel boy, you know. Don't know how but he did.

It was all silly talk, the secret fears of this close-knit community surfacing. In their shocked grief they needed a scapegoat and Kroll had been their bogey man for a long time, because he kept to himself, was an eccentric. In the towns and cities there were dozens like him, the only difference being that they went unnoticed.

The doctor had a ready-made excuse for visiting Kroll. A recent directive from the Medical Association urged GPs to keep a close check on the elderly, especially during the winter months; the usual procedure was to mail them an appointment card, requesting them to call for an annual check-up. If they ignored the invitation then there was little else one could do. Kroll would most certainly ignore his so there was no point in writing to him. The only other alternative was an impromptu call.

Dr King huddled in the turned-up collar of his checked overcoat and turned his back on the icy wind which gusted down the Narrows. He never wore a hat, his unruly shock of grey hair was almost weatherproof.

His third knocking on the door was both loud and decisive, echoing his intolerance. He never liked being kept waiting, oft times when calling on a patient he just walked into the house. Nobody had ever challenged him.

He gripped the tarnished doorknob, turned it, pushed. Weatherworn as the door was, it was clearly locked, probably bolted, too.

'These guys wear braces and a belt!' he muttered irritably to himself. 'The bloody place is like Fort Knox!' In which case he might need help if he had to force an entry. Mr Penry, the ironmonger, would assist him, he had no doubt about that; unquestioningly, the fellow would bring all the necessary tools, have the door, or a window, open in a trice. Penry had helped him to break into old Mrs

Waterson's cottage the winter before last; they had found the old lady dead on the kitchen floor. She had been there almost a week, according to the pathologist. King knew that the policeman had seen Edward Kroll only a matter of a couple of days ago, but it only took a second to die.

'Either dead or bloody deaf!' The doctor glanced towards the ironmongery across the road from the clocktower, glimpsed Mr Penry through the window. He'd give him a shout if there was no answer from Kroll after another couple of minutes.

At that moment King heard footsteps and somebody inside struggling to turn the key.

'Yes?' There was hostility in Edward Kroll's expression and posture as if he thought it was kids knocking his door again.

'Dr King, here.' An abrupt introduction whilst at the same time sliding a foot into the gap in case the door should be suddenly slammed shut.

'Yes?'

A bloody 'yes' man, obviously, King smiled wryly. 'I don't think we've actually met, Mr Kroll, although you are on my list of patients.' He extended a hand.

Surprised, Kroll accepted the gesture. Dr King winced at the touch, its limpness. Like a fillet of plaice from the freezer that had just finished thawing out.

'I didn't send for you, doctor.' Phlegm rattled, the dark eyes looked feverish, filmed over with suspicion.

'I mightn't've come if you had, I'm like that, bloody stubborn!' King laughed at his joke because the other man almost certainly would not. 'It's brass monkeys standing out here in the street.'

'I can't stand here indefinitely with the door open, doctor, it's letting all the heat out of the house.'

'Then invite me in and shut the bloody door, that way we'll both be warmer.' *I have doubts about you, though, mate, you're just like you've come off a mortician's slab.* Mervyn King pushed gently against the door with his shoulder, he was going to take a looksee in here, with or without Kroll's invitation.

'Book collecting is a hobby of mine, too.' The doctor

needed to entice his patient on to common ground; it was too gloomy in this passageway for him to be able to read what was written on either the boxes or the spines of the books stacked above them.

'Oh, that's most interesting.' Kroll's enthusiasm came with a spasm of coughing. 'What genre, doctor?'

'Medical books mostly, some biographies. And literature, too.'

'Dull as ditchwater, boring to read and a complete waste of time. Haven't you yet discovered the delights of boys' adventure stories, doctor? My own collection of books goes from Biggles back to Ranger Gull. The story papers are the finest example of this type of yarn, though. *Adventure*, *Hotspur*, *Rover*, *Wizard*, *Champion* and as far back as the early *Boys' Own* and *Detective Weekly*. And if you wish to read more deeply, try the pulps, pre-war era, naturally. I have amassed complete runs of some titles. I'm really surprised that, as a man of learning, you haven't yet discovered these. Medical books are only fit for salvage, most biographies are uninteresting, with the odd exception, of course. H. P. Lovecraft springs to mind.'

'I've read Lovecraft, years ago.' *God, the place stank like a bloody tomb! The windows hadn't been opened for years, probably.*

'Have you read *The Tomb*?'

Mervyn King shuddered uncontrollably. 'Er, yes, of course.' *But don't bloody ask me anything about it, for Christ's sake.*

'Perhaps we could go and sit down in my living quarters? Straight through that door at the end of the passage.'

Bloody incredible, the place defied belief! King had thought that maybe the police officer had been exaggerating. God, the tea itself was enough to rot your guts, no wonder Kroll was in the state he was.

'We check up on all our senior patients these days,' King said and pretended to take another sip out of politeness. 'It isn't necessary for them to visit the surgery, I'm quite happy to call upon them. You seem to have a chill, Mr Kroll, perhaps a touch of bronchitis.'

'All my Lovecrafts are in these *Weird Tales*,' Kroll said as he reached down to a pile of plastic bagged pulps, handling each one with reverence, like he was showing off a batch of holiday snaps. 'Now, look at that for artwork, a classic Libouski cover.'

King found himself shying from the skull cover, it might have been a photograph of Edward Kroll staring up at him out of eyeless sockets.

'And this Giunta artwork, absolutely out of this world.'

Which it certainly was.

Kroll's lungs were rattling, again he bent double as the coughing took him.

'I really think that I should examine you, Mr Kroll.'

Kroll paused in the act of extolling another example of weird artwork. His expression turned to surprise, he stared. 'What for?'

'Because I think you're ill. In fact, I know you are. If I don't treat you with antibiotics very soon, you'll get pneumonia. Then it'll be hospital. Or worse.'

'I would utterly refuse to go to hospital!' A moment of senile petulance, one of the magazines was slapped angrily on the table. 'You have no right . . .'

'Absolutely none.' King's irascible temper was evident in a reddening of his ears. 'I couldn't force you to go to hospital against your will, just as I can't make you be examined. I'm suggesting it for your own good.'

'A doctor hasn't examined me for thirty years!'

'I can quite believe that!' King shrugged his shoulders. 'I can see I'm wasting my time here.'

'*Wasting your time*?' Kroll shrieked, indicating the pulps on the table, the shelves of books. 'How can anybody waste their time here?'

'Everybody to their own taste,' the doctor said as he rose to his feet.

'You fetched me from my bed!' An accusation.

'So you *are* ill?'

'*Ill*? Of course not, mostly I sleep in the daytime, except on Tuesdays and Thursdays when I venture out at lunchtime for sustenance. The night hours are when I am able to concentrate best, for reading and sorting my collection. In winter, some days I don't get up at all, it saves on the heating bills.'

Mervyn King shook his head in disbelief.

'That policeman sent you, didn't he?' It was almost a scream, a finger stabbed and Kroll almost overbalanced. 'He sent you to pry!'

'I came of my own accord!' King's ears were a dark hue now, his moustache seemed to bristle. 'I came although I didn't have to. I haven't examined you and clearly I won't be able to, but I must warn you that my cursory observations already tell me that you are seriously ill. I can only advise you, warn you. By ignoring your condition, you risk *dying*!'

'I am not afraid of death.' Kroll's hiss came out with a spray of frothy spittle.

'Neither am I,' the doctor said tersley, 'but I'm not ready to go yet. Anyway, please yourself. If you change your mind, call me.'

'It is unlikely!' Arrogantly, proudly.

Because I don't like talking to people.

'You could always come down to the surgery. Mornings, nine to ten, evenings, five to six. Or just ring the bell any time.'

King began walking back down the ill-lit passageway, hearing Kroll's laboured breathing as he watched from the kitchen doorway. The cold atmosphere was stifling with its varied foul stenches: a mustiness that came from damp walls and old books; stale cigarette smoke; unwashed clothes. And something else . . .

Familiar, yet it eluded him until he was back outside, breathing deeply of the fresh mountain air. It was possibly his imagination, the atmosphere was conducive to it. A smell which every doctor knew, lived with, week in week out.

The smell of death.

Seven

'Well, neither sight nor sound of Kroll for a whole week!' There was no mistaking the relief in Christine Morgan's voice as she looked into the dining room where her husband was busy clearing tables.

It had been an unusually busy lunchtime, boosted by a gathering of insurance company representatives who had chosen to eat in the Grillhouse.

'Kroll's absence certainly increases trade,' Christine remarked as she went through to help John.

'We were lucky,' he said as he piled plates on top of one another. 'A reps' lunch, they'd've come in whether Kroll had been here or not because they're strangers. Tomorrow we'll probably not see a soul between half one and three.'

'Well, he must have got the message,' she said with a smile, 'and I don't care if we never see him again.'

'He's probably in bed with flu.'

'And his cottage pie and pud meanwhile are going mouldy in his sandwich box but he'll heat it up and eat it all the same when he's better. And then he'll be ill with food poisoning. So we still won't see him back here.'

'That's vindictive,' John said hesitantly. 'I think maybe I should go and check that he's OK.'

'Don't you bloody dare!' She shook a finger at him. 'He's not our problem.'

'I think I ought to, Chrissie. Mean and nasty as he is, he's spent money here that has helped us in hard times.'

'On cut-price meals!' Her cheeks flushed out a mass of freckles. 'Like I said, Kroll's not our worry, John, we don't owe him a thing. Especially after what he's done to Rick and Tom.'

'The boys seem to have come out of their depression.' He put the dirty plates in the sink. 'They seem OK to me.'

'On the surface.'

'What d'you mean?'

'Admittedly, now that half-term is over, they're back into school routine. But they go the long way round to school so that they don't have to walk past *his* house. And that goes for a number of other folks, too, John. Mothers walking their kids to school go all the way round West Street and into Market Street. And maybe you've noticed how a few regulars have stopped coming in here for coffee. Aggie and Barbara for a start, because they're scared to go near Kroll's house and it's too far to walk round by Market Street. So they use the Clocktower or maybe Ginger's. Kroll's cost us more money than ever he's paid us, and if he never comes back then we're well rid of him. But that's nothing compared with what he's done to Rick and Tom. I'm worried about them. Christ only knows what's going on inside their minds, what effect it will have on them in the future.'

He nodded. Now that she mentioned it he realized that Aggie and Barbara had not been in for at least a week, Frank Wright, too. John had been trying to kid himself that everything was fine now. It clearly was not. Nevertheless, somebody ought to go and check on Edward Kroll for humanitarian reasons. Maybe PC Morris would call in for a coffee one of these days . . .

'I'll have to force an entry . . .' There was a note of resignation in PC Phil Morris's voice. Up until now he had hoped that his persistent knocking would have brought shuffling footsteps to the door. But his pounding fists would have awoken even the heaviest sleeper or been heard above the noise of a radio or television.

From within Kroll's house there was only an unbroken silence.

'My middle name is Sykes,' the sardonic Dr Mervyn King said and felt a craving for a pipe of tobacco but his blackened briar and pouch were on the desk in his study. 'Lead on, prisons these days are as good as retirement homes, so they tell me.'

They were standing in the yard at the rear of the house, an area paved with flat stones around which almost every species of weed known to the horticulturist grew. They had attempted to peer in through the kitchen window but a combination of grime and condensation obscured their view. Up above them the curtains were closed on every window.

'The door will suffice,' Phil said as he pulled on the loose knob, the structure rattling perilously. Once there had been a pane of glass but it had been replaced by an ill-fitting square of chipboard. 'Stand back, doctor!'

The doorknob and lock were ripped away, the door jerked outwards, leaning precariously on a single hinge from which the screws hung out of rotten woodwork.

'No trouble there,' the officer said and then hesitated as that now familiar stale smell seeped out.

Dr King anticipated the stench of death, it did not necessarily mean the worst. 'After you, constable.' This was now a police matter, the medic was only here in case he was needed.

Phil stepped inside, fumbled his way along the wall until his fingers located a greasy light switch. Low wattage light from a dusty, unshaded bulb flooded the porch. Boxes, stacked one upon another, shaky handwriting designating the contents; books and more books.

'The original bookworm,' the constable muttered, feeling a need to say something. 'If you lived to be a hundred you'd never read this lot.'

'Collectors don't read most of what they buy,' King answered. 'It's like collecting stamps, the pleasure of owning something rare.'

'Beats me. Well, he's not in the kitchen.' The adjacent door was open, Phil flicked on the light, left it burning. 'Sixty-watt bulbs all through the house, I guess.'

The doctor ran his hand over an old-fashioned radiator in the hallway where the stack of books continued. 'And no heating at all. My guess is that we'll find him in bed, saving on the electricity bill.'

There were books piled on every stair, neatly arranged, spines outward so that the titles could be read. 'In strict author alphabetical order,' King commented as he bent to peer at a stack of volumes. 'Methodical, to say the least. It's an illness, you know, hoarding things and keeping everything in neat piles, he even keeps his jars of preserves and his loose coins like that. Doubtless there's a hundred other things all systematically arranged throughout the house. It stems from depression in the first place, gets out of hand. Curable, though, provided the patient admits to having a problem and is willing to be treated. Kroll isn't agreeable to any kind of treatment, I offered it to him. He refused.'

Phil Morris guessed he was on the landing because the floor beneath his feet levelled out. Otherwise, he would not have known. Boxes were stacked now so that they formed passageways, in places one had to shuffle sideways. He used his torch, the landing light was masked by the edifice of cartons.

The first passageway led directly to the lavatory, a cracked pan with the seat raised. Kroll was definitely not in there.

'At least he baths.' Morris investigated the next cardboard corridor, his torch beam reflected on a couple of inches or so of greyish cold water. 'He obviously didn't drain it the last time.'

'Another saving on electricity.' Even King's dry humour seemed sinister. 'Or else he's got a phobia about drowning.'

The first bedroom was, predictably, full of books. Shelving this time, doubtless a cut-price job because the wood had been neither planed nor varnished. Each shelf was labelled with stick-on labels that the damp was furling.

'We have to find him soon, doctor. *If* he's home.'

The only closed door leading off from this warren-like landing faced them, an off-white that seemed to glow in the half light.

'He'll be in there,' King whispered.

'I guess so.' Phil's outstretched hand closed, he almost knocked instinctively. He was grateful to Dr King for coming along.

A scratching and scurrying made them both start. King

said, 'Mice, the place is doubtless over-run with them.' He knew that his companion needed to hear another human voice.

The door swung open with surprising ease, the hinges did not even squeal. The stygian blackness beyond seemed to come at them, they felt its iciness prickling their skin and turned their heads away from the stench which was a hundred times stronger than the one downstairs. It was cloying; they tasted it and wanted to vomit, gasping for breath and drawing more into their lungs. It was as though they had chanced upon the den of some animal, a lair that stank of excrement and urine, an unwashed body that sweated and dried and never washed.

Edward Kroll was where they expected to find him, sitting up in bed.

The only item of furniture beside the ancient iron bedstead was a small chest of drawers. On it stood a red thermos flask and a Tupperware box with the lid off; it was from this that the stench of putrefaction came.

Anywhere else but here, Edward Kroll might have seemed comical. The bedsheets had been thrown back, he sat upright with legs splayed, a striped nightshirt attempting to hide his frailty. His arms were held wide, puny fists clenched. His head was back, hatless and resting on the iron structure at the rear.

His eyes were open, dull and watching their every move, a scowling rictus that was angered at this instrusion upon his privacy. Nostrils flared, clogged with mucus, some of it had dripped and stained the material of his night attire a yellowish green before it dried.

'Jesus!' Phil Morris stepped back on to Dr King's foot but the other did not seem to notice. Both of them, familiar with death, fought and overcame an urge to flee.

Within seconds Mervyn King was the professional GP again, pushing his way past the police officer, making a swift examination of the unholy figure on the bed.

When he turned back he was decisive, brusque. 'He's been dead some time, maybe two or three days. You'd best report it to Llandrindod, I'll call the morticians, get them to fetch the body in. There's no point in us staying here any longer.'

A routine procedure, an anti-climax because Dr King made it that way for the benefit of the young constable. They hurried from the house of death because there was work to be done, neither would have admitted to any other cause for haste.

They stumbled on the stairway, because the books were an obstacle to their departure. Hurrying along the narrow passageway, because the stench was overpowering and their lungs wheezed for fresh air. Dragging the broken door shut after them, in case vandals or thieves found a way inside.

Or in case Edward Kroll rose from his bed and walked the streets again.

Eight

The mortuary in town had been owned by the Pohl family through succeeding generations, right back to the days when it had been a charnel house. It had been moved from its original site, burned down, rebuilt and, in recent years, extended to accommodate an increasing and, subsequently, dying population. But, in spite of modernization, death was much the same as it had been centuries hence. Natural or accidental, swift or lingering, a corpse was a corpse, as Victor Pohl never ceased to remind the regulars in the George and Dragon.

Victor Pohl drank one pint of Guinness on week nights, two on Saturdays and abstained on the Sabbath because chapel and booze were a contradiction. A kind of self-sacrifice, just as his father and grandfather before him had done. He believed in tradition, it was part of religion if you thought about it.

He would be sixty-five in January and eligible for a pension, but he had no intention of retiring. His father had worked right up to the end of his days, collapsing after old John Lewis's funeral, and Victor had gone straight back to the the mortuary and laid him out. And made a real fine job of it, too. At eighty-nine, Eli Pohl had looked younger than John Lewis had done and he'd been ninety-four. Corpses were as old, or as young, as you made 'em look.

Gallons of stout over the years had not put an ounce of surplus flesh on Victor's lean frame. A man of meticulous cleanliness, he donned a fresh suit of bib overalls daily, except for funerals when he wore a grey morning suit and a top hat to match. That was tradition, too.

He tried to hide his baldness by brushing strands of his

thinning grey hair across it. His expression was of an habitual sombreness, perfected over the years into a gloominess that had forgotten how to smile even when the bereaved paid promptly with a sizeable cheque. Hand-made coffins were a rarity in this age of mass production, a dying art; he mumbled a laugh at his long played out joke without somehow managing to smile, dislodging the ash from the eternal cigarette that smouldered in the centre of his lips and often rendered his speech inaudible.

'Kroll's dead!'

Victor Pohl made the announcement from the bar in the George and Dragon where Frank Minton, the licencee, had brought him the cordless phone. Dr King brusquely ordered Victor to go and fetch the body in from the Narrows, his repartee with the town's undertaker was laced with expletives that had a decidedly edgy ring to them. But, then, King was on the brink of retirement, he had every right to be pissed off with corpses on a rainy November evening.

Victor perched on his high stool and swung round to face the crowded bar. They were making such a bloody row with their chattering that they hadn't even heard him! He drew breath for a louder shout, saw that the town crier was amongst the gathering, come straight in for a pint from his building job. Well, this was going to be one up on *him*!

'*Oi*!'

Little Larry looked round from his seat at the far end of the bar. He was ninety-two and showed no signs of becoming a customer down at the mortuary, his hearing was as acute as that of a man half his age. He was nudging those around him, pointing in Victor's direction. The conversation died away in stages like a fall of dominoes.

'Take yer bloody fag out of yer mouth then we'll be able to 'ear you!'

With as much dignity as he could muster, Victor Pohl took the cigarette from between his lips. He cleared his throat. The others waited, humoured him, the town crier whispered something to a fellow drinker.

'Come on, then, let's 'ear it!'

'I said . . .' Victor took a deep breath, let it out slowly, yelling in a voice that came out high-pitched, '*Kroll's dead*!'

The silence was absolute, it was as if everybody in the small bar was frozen into immobility, trapped in their last action: glasses suspended, raised or lowered; Larry's tilted, poured a steady stream of Welsh Bitter into his lap but he did not appear to notice. The town crier's mouth hung open but there was no *oyez* forthcoming. The pint that Frank Minton was drawing overfilled the glass and ran to waste down the sink beneath.

Then, very slowly, the room came back to life. Drinkers looked at one another, shocked expressions, disbelief. Larry checked his spill, took a gulp.

'*Kroll's dead*!' Victor's announcement seemed to echo round the bar, vibrating in numbed brains.

Then excited, deafening chatter broke out. Victor was forgotten, the news was broken and it mattered not who had broken it.

Edward Kroll was dead and it was a matter for rejoicing.

So *that* was Kroll! Victor stared in sheer amazement at the naked corpse on the slab.

'He's no bigger than a bloody *babby*!' The mortician's surprised exclamation dislodged half an inch of ash from his habitual cigarette on to the stretched membraneous flesh, an unintended gesture of contempt. 'Gruesome, ain't yuh?' He poked at the body, it was taut and springy, cold as ice, which it was bound to be. All the same, he experienced an unaccustomed feeling of revulsion for one who had spent a lifetime tending the dead. He glanced around nervously, it didn't seem as brightly lit in here as it usually was, maybe there had been another of those all too frequent reductions in voltage. He'd a good mind to phone the electricity board. Tomorrow, of course, he was too busy right now.

A loud expellation of wind made Victor jump, a moment of fear that passed as quickly as it had come. Dead bodies often released a pocket of wind that had become trapped inside them.

'You dirty old bugger!' The crudity was forced, a cover-up for his uneasiness. One needed a sense of humour if one was to retain sanity when most of the time your only company was the deceased. 'No bloody manners, that's your trouble. I've 'eard all about you rippin' 'em off in the Grillhouse!'

Kroll appeared to be staring balefully at him, angry because he had been ridiculed. Well, *that* was soon rectified! Victor delved into a side pocket of his overalls, something clinked. He leaned over the body and pulled the eyelids down and weighted them with a couple of fifty-pence coins. He should have done that in the beginning, for some reason tonight he had overlooked it.

'There, now you've got no option but to mind your own bleedin' business! What I do 'as got nuffin' whatever to do wiv you. Get it?' He had a slight impediment of speech that was most noticeable when he was nervous. 'Just you lie still, leave it all to me and I'll 'ave you fixed in no time at all.' It was bloody stupid chatting to a corpse but there wasn't anybody else around to talk to and the sound of his own voice was somehow reassuring. Well, just a little.

Kroll's mouth seemed to tighten, an expression of disapproval. Just the nerves, they reacted in different ways, either tightened or loosened. Victor had witnessed it many times before. He had also heard of headless cockerels running round a farmyard until their nerves gave out.

Nevertheless, his uneasiness was mounting. But he wasn't scared of a little 'un like Kroll, no way.

'You're *nothin*.' He began to wash the naked flesh, wrinkling his nose at patches of grime that a couple of inches of bathwater hadn't reached. 'Never was, and you certainly ain't now!'

Dr King should have done a PM, it wasn't like him to duck it. All the doctor had given Kroll's body was a cursory examination, diagnosed bronchial pneumonia. Sure, that was what had finished Kroll off, lots of old people snuffed it that way, pneumonia set in once they took to their bed, but there was undoubtedly something much more serious festering in that tiny, wasted body. Cancer, probably. Maybe the doc thought it was irrelevant, so long as no foul play was suspected he was on reasonably safe ground.

Pity, Victor could have used the PM fee; held the bucket whilst King dropped all the bits and pieces into it, handed them back when he was finished cutting and delving. Sometimes the doctor left the undertaker to stich the corpse up again, tipped him an extra fiver for it. Nobody ever found out, you made sure the shroud was in place and that relatives who came for a last look didn't go poking around. A bloke could really enjoy an extra Guinness earned that way and a pack of fags to go with it.

The doc was sure easing up in his last year, and who could blame him. There, that's about as clean as I can get this old fucker and what the hell does it matter? They should've cremated him, burned the bleedin' lot!

The lights flickered again. Victor started at the sink, hoped there wasn't going to be a power failure. Normally, the dark didn't worry him. *Normally.*

A loud ripping noise, the bugger'd blown off again. What Kroll had done in life, he was doing in death.

Victor could have left the rest of the work until morning except that Reuben, his assistant, was off sick and there were two funerals, one at eleven and another at twelve thirty. Old folks; once November came with its damp and fogs, business looked up.

There was a kids' coffin left in the storehouse that would fit Edward Kroll; Victor always kept one in stock, hoping not to use it. It brought back sad memories even for one whose living came from death.

'They're a lot of silly scared buggers in this town,' he said with a cracked voice, almost an apology. 'Never 'eard anything like it, saying Kroll had killed the Farrell boy. 'Ow could 'e when 'e never stepped outside 'is 'ouse? If there'd been an earthquake like that one a few years ago, they'd've blamed 'im for that, too. Me, I don't hold with that sort of malicious gossip and if I 'ear anybody sayin' . . .'

A sudden groan, a high pitched wheeze vibrated an atmosphere that seemed to have gone ten degrees colder. Victor Pohl had been in the act of pulling a small coffin down off the top of a stack of larger ones; his hand jerked, the coffin tilted, slid, avalanched those beneath it.

Victor leaped out of the way just in time. Polished wooden casks showered, piled, rolled in all directions. Victor's shriek, muffled by the lips that closed over his cigarette, was drowned in the crashings. The lights flickered again.

And then went out.

The mortician stood there in the unyielding darkness, not so much as a sliver of street lighting filtered through the shuttered windows. He drew on his cigarette, coughed and heard it echo eerily. He was shaking but that was probably due to physical exertion. Not fear; he wasn't scared of *anything*.

The sudden fall of coffins, the loss of the lighting, disoriented him. It was silly but he could not work out exactly where the doorway was. It had to be over there, to his left.

It wasn't; his outstretched fingers met with a cold brick wall. Which wall? The one on the right or the left? It didn't matter, all he had to do was to follow it round and in due course he would arrive at the exit. He needed to get out of here, because you couldn't work in the dark, could you?

That's it, keep going, feel your way and mind the cupboard. There wasn't a cupboard, it had to be against the opposite wall, which meant that any second he'd come upon the desk where he did his paperwork.

There wasn't any desk.

Something was wrong, whichever wall he was following, in whatever direction, he must reach the door eventually. He sensed a flicker of panic, fought it off. He'd worked in this place all his life, trained as an apprentice to his father, knew every square inch of it.

He obviously didn't.

Maybe Reuben had looked in earlier, moved a few things round. He wouldn't do that, he did as little as possible even when he was in good health.

Something touched Victor.

He whirled around but the blackness was too intense, not so much as an outline showed.

'Who's there?'

A wheeze from diseased, dead lungs answered him.

Victor might have screamed except that no sound came from his dry lips; a soggy cigarette bobbed up and down on them.

'That you, Reuben?' Reuben wouldn't come here outside working hours, it was job enough to get him here during them. It was a bloody silly question asked as a final resort.

Victor was aware how his long winter underpants clung wetly to his legs with a warmth that was in contrast to the icyness elsewhere. His bald pate goosepimpled.

He brushed against something hard and cold; the marble slab upon which he prepared the bodies for burial. He shied away from it, his instinct was to flee blindly. Instead, he stretched out a shaking hand, slid his fingers along the smooth surface. Only minutes ago he had been attending to Kroll upon it.

A rasping cancerous cough came from close by. Edward Kroll had to be lying upon it, his emaciated body getting rid of all its surplus air in a variety of ways. Feeling for Kroll, searching for him with a hand that shook uncontrollably.

Edward Kroll was not there.

That was when Victor Pohl broke into a stumbling, panic-stricken run in an attempt to find a way out of this place.

It was as though freezing fingers reached out to hinder his progress. He bumped against a chair, sent it spinning, kicked an object that skated across the stone floor, bounced off a wall.

Rasping laughter that might have been a gust of November wind rattling the door. Something touched him again, snatched its hand away. He fled in the opposite direction, wet his underwear a second time.

And then the lights came back on and found him cowering, dazzled, up against the door which he had been trying to locate. He stared with frightened eyes; apart from the mountain of fallen coffins that blocked the doorway through to the storeroom, everything was as it should have been.

Edward Kroll was lying stiffly on the marble slab, looking

up at the ceiling with grotesque octaganal orbe. Just where he should have been. Except that . . . *He lay facing in the opposite direction.*

The Reverend Albert Crawford had been offered a 'quiet' parish a few years back, a way of retiring him with dignity. He had refused adamantly, he would accept that diplomatic diocesan offer when *he* considered that the time was right, and not until. White hair, a shuffling walk and failing eyesight did not mean that one was not fit to carry out. God's work. It was spiritual, not physical, strength that counted.

Today, though, was a strain. These townspeople were soaked in their own maliciousness, not a single one of them had turned out to pay their last respects to one who had lived amongst them for many years, albeit as a recluse. Instead, they had shut themselves away in their homes, continued their whispering campaign behind closed and, possibly, bolted doors.

Today was bitterly cold and the fog had rolled back down from the mountains, crept through the streets and up towards the church as if it was escorting the cortege, trying to hide the shame of a community that gloated over the death of one of their own.

There was no congregation apart from Victor Pohl and his professional mourners. No organist because the funeral service would be spoken, not sung. The gravediggers lurked somewhere in the thickening mist, the vicar sensed their presence even though they were not visible.

The service had lasted less than a quarter of an hour. How could one give an address when one knew nothing whatsoever about the deceased?

The mortician and his colleagues had retired to the back of the church, at one stage Crawford thought that they had left. Just his own cracked tones rasped down the aisle, whispering echoes up in the rafters.

'Man that is born of woman hath but a short time to live and is full of misery. O holy and most merciful Saviour, deliver us not into the pains of eternal death.'

Eternal death.

The ropes took the strain of the coffin as it bumped its way down into the grave. Crawford noticed how Victor Pohl stood back, seemed to shy from the burial.

'Ashes to ashes, dust to dust.'

The coffin grated on the bottom. With seemingly undue haste, the ropes were pulled back, the bearers' feet padded down the pathway towards the street.

The vicar bowed his head, muttered a final prayer. Lord have mercy upon thy poor servant who has suffered the hatred of his fellow men and help them to repent of their wickedness.

The gravediggers emerged from the fog, set about the task of filling in the grave, working with a zest which might have been a desire to be finished and away from this cold, fogbound place.

Or maybe they were desperate to bury a curse that had been amongst them for as long as they could remember, be rid of it forever in eternal death.

Nine

'We don't know any more about the man now that he's dead than we did when he was alive,' George Edmonds, the lawyer, announced as he turned back from the window, held up a wallet file and dropped it on to his desk. 'The only link we have with Kroll is through the bank, a bank statement that shows a considerable balance. Add to that the contents of his house and, pending a bookdealer's valuation of his books, the guy was worth a small fortune. The deeds of his house have so far not turned up. He's probably got them hidden away somewhere in the house and I'm hoping that they will be found and, hopefully, we'll find a will, too. If we don't, then he's died intestate and it'll take years to sort out his affairs. I was just hoping that you might be able to shed a little light on the mystery, Mervyn. Anything you might know about Kroll will be invaluable to us.'

Mervyn King sat awkwardly in the chair on the other side of the desk. Lawyers' offices were not conducive to his abrupt, if strangely reassuring beside manner, his own inimitable charisma. He seemed embarrassed, shook his head slowly, looked at the tall man with the flowing beard. Giants within a community that they had made their own domain, they shared a seemingly unsolvable problem.

'It would be an insult for me to suggest that you contacted the National Registry of Births and Deaths', King said hesitantly, 'just as it would be for you to recommend that I took aspirin for a headache.' He took his cue from the other's cigarette to produce his pipe and, stuffed the blackened bowl with coarse stranded tobacco.

'They appear to have mislaid the relevant documentation,'

Edmonds said with a sigh as he lowered himself into his chair, crossing one long leg over the other. 'Which is the first time in thirty years that I've had any problem with them over a routine enquiry. They infer that *we* might have made a mistake, got the name wrong. However, they're still searching and will contact me again. Which means a wait of twenty-eight days and then they'll say they can't find any trace of the birth certificate.'

'I only ever met him twice.' King got his pipe drawing to his satisfaction. 'On the second occasion he was dead.'

'I've asked Addenbrook, the antiquarian bookseller from Oxford, to come up this week and attempt to value the books.' Edmonds pursed his lips. 'That'll be costly but at least it's a step forward. One thing I'd like to know, who the bloody hell *was* Edward Kroll?'

'Nobody in town knows.' The doctor seemed uncharacteristically uneasy. 'He just appeared. Nobody can remember when and they don't want to. They were terrified of him, and since that unfortunate road accident they're blaming him for everything that's happened over the last twenty-five years. Some sick idiots have daubed graffiti on his front door.'

'I've seen it. "Murderer".'

'Maybe they're trying to get him out of their system, laying a bogeyman. If it stops at graffiti, that's fine. I suggested to the police that they keep an eye on his house.'

'Books are no good to burglars unless they're well read and there's precious little else in the place.'

'I'm not worried about burglars, I don't think any of the locals would set foot in Kroll's house. Arson is a possibility.'

'And as far as I can ascertain, Kroll never insured his premises, but I guess it's no good worrying about it.' Edmonds stretched his legs, stood up. 'I guess the outcome will be that the state coffers will be swelled from the sale of the hoardings of a miserly recluse. In due course some outsider will buy the house and maybe in years to come the townsfolk will forget all about Edward Kroll.'

'I doubt they'll ever forget him.' Mervyn King knocked

out his pipe in the ashtray. 'He'll be the bogeyman of Knighton for years to come.'

On the following Monday morning Ralph Addenbrook arrived in town and checked in at the Red Lion hotel. A stranger always attracted curiosity in a remote rural township and none more so than the tall, florrid-faced man who created an instant air of affluence with his silver Mercedes and his expensively tailored suit.

Ralph Addenbrook's only interest in life was books, not in their content, that was irrelevant, but in their value. He impressed upon the staff of his three antiquarian bookshops that a book was worth what it would sell for, a yardstick he had used since his teenage days when he had opened a small second-hand shop on London's Portobello Road.

He had progressed from there to postal selling; he exploited the merits of an expensively produced catalogue, cheap duplicated lists bespoke tatty books. The term 'scarce' was a lure to the speculator and the investor. A high price denoted rarity, condition was then of secondary importance. Specialization was the key to success, general bookshops were little better than market stalls.

He was a man who had found his niche in life and had become respected throughout the worldwide book trade. Valuations were expensive but his reputation ensured that he was in constant demand. None questioned his pricings, it would not have been in their interest to devalue a worthwhile collection.

Often his expenses exceeded his fee, he was a man who enjoyed the best things in life. He had booked en suite accommodation because he expected the job, from what Edmonds had told him, to take several days; to have completed it in less would have made his fee seem extortionate.

'The house is full of books from attic to ground floor, many of them boxed,' Edmonds explained as he unlocked the front door and switched on the hall light. 'Every box is labelled.'

'Which will be impossible to read without better light.'

Addenbrook exaggerated his squint. 'I can't work in *that*, a candle would be better!'

'I'll get the bulbs changed,' the lawyer offered hastily. 'There's an electrician down the street, I'll see if he can do it.'

'Thank you, I'll go back to the hotel for half an hour whilst he fixes it.' The bookdealer turned away. The sight and smell of the interior of that hovel had nauseated him, for a moment he considered changing his mind but he was a man of his word and it would undoubtedly have tarnished his reputation.

He could taste that stench. He ordered a pot of strong coffee to be brought up to his room in an attempt to cleanse his palate. On reflection, if the contents of each box was written on it, perhaps he could work from that information. A man as fastidious as the previous owner would undoubtedly be particular concerning condition and Addenbrook could always check the odd carton at random.

It was midday by the time Edmonds telephoned the Red Lion to report that every light fitting in the house now had a 100-watt bulb; he had also turned on the heating. Addenbrook ordered a light lunch, he would make a start afterwards. There was no hurry now that he had decided upon a modus opperandi that would simplify and speed up his task.

Somehow, even the more powerful bulbs appeared dim but that was due to the dark-brown decor and the fact that the stacked boxes restricted the light. And if the heating had been switched on then it was having little effect, probably because the house was damp after being unoccupied for a couple of weeks. Well, he'd work for a couple of hours, return in the morning.

Within half an hour Ralph Addenbrook was fully aware of the value of the hallway books. This man, Kroll, had to be crazy; he had amassed a valuable collection of early consecutive runs of Victorian Penny Dreadfuls and then the next section was devoted to cheap pocket reprints of well-known classics, the kind that every bookshop accumulated but were only too happy to off-load on to the local charity shops or send for re-cycling.

There was no pattern to the deceased's collecting mania: a box of paperback romances, some non-fiction works on fox-hunting that would have commanded a high price and yet could not possibly have been of any interest to a recluse. Undoubtedly, the entire stock of books needed sorting into categories, the rubbish needed dumping and the rest going to auction. That was the only way they could be sold. But it was too early yet, probate might not be granted for months. Edmonds merely needed a total figure to compile Kroll's assets. Then, perhaps a sale might be considered.

Addenbrook's eyes narrowed, he stared in almost disbelief at a near fine copy of Nimrod's *Memoirs of the Life of John Mytton,* an 1837 second edition. A price was pencilled in the flyleaf; £2.75. Dear God, I don't believe it! He gazed with reverence at the coloured etchings, a puff of dust had him sneezing. One of the rarest of all hunting books, featuring the legendary 'Mad Jack Mytton' whom it was said went duck-hunting in the nude on freezing moonlit nights and overturned his carriage deliberately to show his passenger, a cleric, how it was done! A madman who womanized and kept a bear as a pet. And Edward Kroll, a different kind of madman, had picked it up for a pittance, probably out of curiosity, and had no idea of its value.

Addenbrook had his brief case with him; the thought was tempting.

A noise that seemed to come from an upper storey had him listening; it did not come again, it was probably a rat, doubtless the place was infested with them. This was another reason why the books should not be left here for too long. The damp was another factor that would hasten deterioration, some of the covers already showed early signs of mould.

Addenbrook placed the valuable tome on top of a box by the door. He would give it further thought, temptation was paramount. If he made an offer for the entire collection, and it was accepted, then the book would be his, anyway. Nobody would miss it in the meantime. He could offer to waive his fee, tempt the solicitor into selling; the fee was derisory by comparison with the profit to be made.

And, anyway, the volume ought to be stored in a place of safety. Edmonds clearly had no knowledge of books, was not interested.

Ralph Addenbrook went upstairs.

A sharp stabbing pain had his hand going to his chest, he was temporarily breathless. Damn it, that moment of excitement had triggered his angina. The pain did not come back; he had some tablets back at the hotel, he would take one immediately upon his return. There was no real cause for concern, it was just that one did not come upon copies of that Nimrod book every day. He only knew of a couple in existence.

He stared in dismay at the piled boxes, the passageways between. There might well be other such rarities in any one of them. It would be a task of no small magnitude to move the cartons just to read the contents listed on them; even in the peak of health and twenty years younger than his fifty-eight, he would have baulked at the task. Far better to examine them at his leisure in the warmth and comfort of his own Oxford premises.

The heating system must have failed altogether. Addenbrook rubbed his hands together, he had failed to notice the drop in temperature in his excitement, it had . . . crept up on him. He shivered, found himself glancing nervously about him. But there was nothing to see except box upon box of books.

The small room was shelved. He ran his eye professionally along the rows of spines, authors and titles. This was mediocre stuff, you priced them at three pounds and hoped for some passing trade during the tourist season. He did not bother checking the far wall.

The door at the far end of the landing was ajar, the light shafted in through it. An iron bedstead made patterned shadows on the far wall, a pillow was propped up as though it had been used as a support.

Kroll died in there.

The thought came unprompted, had Addenbrook backing away. The room smelled, a stench that might have lain in wait for him; an aroma of decomposing matter, almost tangible.

It was probably a dead rat. Somebody might have laid some poisoned bait after Kroll's death, rodents had crawled beneath the floorboards, died and stank until they rotted away.

Or it could be Edward Kroll's own death smell.

Addenbrook didn't need to stay any longer, he had seen all he needed to see. Back in the warmth and safety of his hotel apartment, he would do some costing; double the figure, double it again, deduct his expenses. In the morning he would make Edmonds an offer. With luck he could be back in Oxford by lunchtime. He would instruct one of the drivers to come back to Knighton with the big van later in the week and load up the books. Addenbrook would not accompany him. No way. He never wanted to see this hateful place again.

Somebody was coming up the stairs.

Ralph Addenbrook froze, he was aware of that stench of putrefaction. Of evil. It was vile, growing stronger by the second, seeming to come from every direction.

Another step, a stair creaked. Something scurried; even the rats fled in terror here.

Who's there? Who is it? Addenbrook's words would not come, he mouthed the questions, terrified in case they were answered.

Movement returned to his limbs, his legs were shaking, he might have fled if there had been anywhere to flee to but the only place was that dreadful bedroom that stank of death and evil. His escape route down the stairs was cut off.

He was trapped.

Another sharp jab deep in his chest, he found it difficult to breathe. Whoever was coming upstairs was almost at the landing. Another second and whoever it was would be in full view. Ralph Addenbrook cowered, waited.

You were going to steal the book, weren't you?

No, I swear it!

Liar!

You're going to cheat me out of all my books, aren't you?

No, I don't want them. Let me go, I won't make an offer, I promise.

'Are you all right, Mr Addenbrook?'

If he had not been breathless, Ralph Addenbrook would, in all probability, have screamed. A strangulated gurgle escaped his trembling lips, vaporized in the cold. He slumped up against a stack of boxes, his legs threatened to crumple beneath him.

Footsteps approached, he sensed somebody close behind him. A hand reached out, touched him. His vision clouded, blackness closed in on him. He felt his fingers slipping on the boxes.

Strong hands caught him as he fell, miraculously unconsciousness eluded him. He squinted from beneath half closed eyelids, afraid to look. In case he saw . . .

'Take it easy, you're OK.' The voice was reassuring. Addenbrook risked a look and gasped aloud with sheer relief.

It was George Edmonds.

'I'm all right, really I am, Mr Edmonds,' the bookdealer asserted as he struggled to stand. 'It's the cold, that awful smell.'

'I thought it had warmed up quite well in here.' Edmonds' expression was one of mingled concern and puzzlement. 'I can't smell anything. At least, nothing more than the usual mustiness.'

'I'm OK, really I am.'

'Maybe you'd better call it a day, I'll ask Dr King to check you over.'

'No, no, that won't be necessary, I'm fine. Really, I am.'

Edmonds watched the other carefully, he did seem to have made a remarkable recovery. 'Well, at least go back to the hotel, rest up a while. Maybe we could have a drink and a chat later this evening.'

'Yes, that would be a good idea.' Addenbrook supported himself on the boxes of books and followed his companion back towards the stairway.

You're trying to cheat me out of my books!

He might have rushed for the front door only the lawyer was in his way. He resisted the urge to push him. *We have to get away from here.*

Upstairs something moved, it sounded too heavy for a rat.

Surprisingly it was dusk outside, the sky was clear and it looked as though there might be a frost later.

'I didn't expect you to work so late.' Edmonds locked the door with some difficulty, dropping the key in his pocket. 'I thought I'd better check on you when I saw the lights were still on.'

'I guess I should have left it till tomorrow,' Addenbrook admitted and smiled weakly. 'The drive up here was tiring. I guess I suffered from exhaustion up there on the landing.'

'I'll see you later on.' Edmonds turned away.

Addenbrook stood and watched the lawyer striding away into the gathering dusk. A thought nagged him; with Edmonds' unexpected appearance and that strange experience a few minutes ago, he'd completely forgotten about the book he'd left in the hallway. It was too late now.

You're going to steal my book!

It was as though somebody had spoken right behind him in the street. Addenbrook whirled but there was nobody there. There never had been, his mind had been playing tricks on him all along. That house was weird but he didn't have to go in there again. He could get what he wanted over a brandy in the lounge bar of the Red Lion.

He turned back towards the glowering house and spoke aloud. 'Fuck you!'

'They're mostly run-of-the-mill books.' Ralph Addenbrook sounded plausible, he had dined well and was on his second brandy, a double. His confidence had returned, it was safe and warm in here and the only aroma was the one that seeped through from the kitchen. 'There's some good stuff amongst it, admittedly. The magazines, mostly. The rest is shop stuff, an auction house wouldn't look at it. The guy just hoarded books, obviously didn't know a lot about them. Classics reprints, reading material. Sorry to disappoint you.'

'I'm not really surprised.' Edmonds was clearly disappointed. 'At least I've done my duty, had them looked at.

You haven't put a value on them or do you want a second look tomorrow?'

'No!' Addenbrook hoped his refusal did not sound too emphatic, he'd almost shouted it. 'It would just be wasting my time and your money. In all honesty, I can't really charge you a lot for the valuation, I wouldn't sleep easy in my bed.

I won't, anyway, after *that*.

Edmonds sipped his drink, said, 'I suppose the books will just have to stay where they are. If I can't find a beneficiary I'll have to try to persuade some of the bookshops in the area to take them. Or give them to charity shops. Or something.'

'They're beginning to damp stain badly.' Addenbrook made it sound casual. 'Over at Hay the bookstores have stacks of throw-outs, they sell them in bulk to people with woodstoves.'

'Oh, I see.'

'Like I said, there *is* some good stuff. I'd be interested in that.'

'And maybe I could persuade you to take away the rubbish with them?'

'Perhaps . . .' Addenbrook had long ago perfected his expression of reluctance. 'A couple of grand for the whole show, perhaps.'

'I guess cash is preferable to books slowly rotting away. I'll have to discuss it with my partner in the morning but I don't envisage any problems. Look, I'll call round after breakfast tomorrow.'

'No hurry.' Ralph Addenbrook drained his glass. There was, but he would wait.

Thief!

Fuck you! Addenbrook forced a smile and went across to the bar to order another round.

Norma liked to have the breakfasts finished and the dining room cleared by ten o'clock, especially on Tuesdays because that was her shopping morning. She had become a creature of habit for her own convenience; a trip down to the supermarket, a visit to the hairdresser and she could be back in time to start cooking the early lunches. During the winter months the Red Lion relied upon local professional men and perhaps a few salesmen passing through. Trade was steady, she didn't wish it otherwise even if the boss did.

Blast, that book fellow hadn't come down yet! She glanced at the clock, clicked her tongue in annoyance. Breakfast was from seven thirty to nine thirty, a note on the tariff in the bedrooms advised guests of that. Norma was prepared to be flexible. Except on Tuesdays. It was now five minutes after ten o'clock.

Perhaps Mr Adden . . . or whatever his name was, didn't eat breakfast. Or he'd overslept. She could not remember him asking for a morning call but that was maybe because he'd had too much to drink last night. Or he'd forgotten.

Any other day she would probably have left him to sleep on. But not on a Tuesday. If he wanted a fully-cooked English breakfast there were a couple of rashers of bacon left over, it wouldn't take more than a minute or so to fry an egg. Or maybe he preferred cereal and toast. Whichever, she could not hang on much longer.

She went through to the hallway; Donna, the teenager who came in to clean three times a week, was just starting to vacuum the stairs.

'Donna, go and give a knock on the door of room seven, will you?' She had to shout to make herself heard above the noise of the machine. 'Just tell him it's after ten, and if he wants any breakfast he'd better come downstairs.'

Donna signalled to show that she had heard, took the stairs two at a time.

Norma was impatient, she wanted to get downtown. She began straightening the tourism leaflets in the rack by the door, hoped that their guest would refuse the offer of a late breakfast. He didn't deserve any if he was too sodding lazy to get out of bed.

Damn that girl, she'd left the vacuum running, too bloody idle to switch it off for a minute. Where the hell had she got to? Room seven was only on the first floor, a couple of loud knocks should be enough to rouse the late sleeper. Do you want any breakfast or don't you? No, then that's fine. Hurry up for Christ's sake, Donna, or I'll miss my hair appointment . . .

Then Norma heard Donna screaming hysterically up on the first-floor landing.

Ten

The high stool at the end of the bar in the George and Dragon was traditionally Larry's, just the same today as it had been half a century ago when he had first come to town; five feet high and ninety-two years of age was a combination that commanded respect. On Saturday evenings, even when the bar was crowded to capacity, that seat remained vacant in readiness for Larry's arrival around nine thirty. If by chance a stranger should happen to occupy it, one of the regulars politely explained that it was reserved.

Larry had an air of urgency about him, he had never been any different. He pushed his way through the drinkers, coat folded over his arm, as if he might just be in time for last orders. One risked a sharp rebuke if one offered to help him up on to the stool. Once perched and comfortable, he proceeded to light a cigarette and crane his neck in search of Frank Minton; age jumped the queue, no matter how many drinkers were waiting to be served. If there was any undue delay, Larry rapped on the polished mahogany top with a coin, a noise that somehow penetrated the cacophony of laughter and conversation.

A pint of Welsh bitter and a whisky chaser, his order was a foregone conclusion. Once a temporary barmaid had enquired what he would like, received an abrupt 'the usual'. Larry had repeated his request, stubbornly refused to explain further, and only the intervention of another customer had saved her from a rebuke.

On a shelf below the spirits was a bulk pack of Woodbines; Larry always bought three packs of twenty which lasted him until the following Saturday. No other brand would suffice, certainly he would never smoke 'those new-fangled fags with spats on' so Frank ensured that there was always an adequate supply of Woodbines. Larry refused to buy his smokes from any of the shops in town because beer and fags were inseparable.

Larry was not retired, he made sure that if there were any strangers in the bar they were well aware of that. Sure, the railway had dispensed with his services in 1966 but that was their loss. He tended three gardens in town, mowed the grass in the cemetery in summer and found enough odd jobs to keep him going throughout the winter. And if anybody enquired of his secret for longevity, he would signal for them to place an ear where he could whisper into it, and inform them that if he'd been foolish enough to marry then somebody would have been mowing the grass around *him* by now. Not that he had anything against women, he hastened to add, just in case his throaty whisper should carry to a female ear, but you enjoyed a hassle-free life without them. He wasn't celibate, a wink and a throaty laugh, 'everything' was in perfect working order, but he'd been a little more canny than most men.

Early to bed, early to rise, was another valuable ingredient for a long life, he added. Except Saturday nights and Sunday mornings, one had to make exceptions to any rule. The George and Dragon was his second call, he'd come here from the Jockey. His itinerary never varied; he'd move on to the Plough and then a last drink at the Red Lion. Fish and chips for supper, the chippie kept open till midnight. That accounted for Saturdays and nobody really knew what time he rose on Sundays, that was something which he did not whisper into any ear; everybody was entitled to *one* secret.

Tonight was exceptionally noisy in the bar, it seemed that everybody in town had chosen to drink here in preference to the other six alternatives. Larry's seat was kept vacant pending his arrival, there were no strangers needing to be informed politely that they could not sit there.

Larry would never have admitted to having defective hearing; he complained frequently that others failed to speak clearly. Tonight voices were lowered, there was obviously some issue at stake that was being discussed. He sat there, his eyes roved from face to face, he did not fail to discern the expressions of fear, the way people huddled, cast glances in the direction of the doorway. He pulled his cap down even more firmly on his head, watched stoically. They would not leave him out of an important conversation for long. They would not dare.

'They found the bookman dead in bed this morning,' a balding farmer leaned across and shouted at the top of his voice in Larry's ear.

Everybody stopped talking, heads were turned. The tension was akin to that of a fused bomb, you braced yourself for the explosion because it was too late to run.

'Eh?' Either Larry had not heard or else he wasn't concentrating. It came as an anti-climax, somebody at the back of the room whispered something. Say it again, Joe, so that we can all hear. We know what you said but we want to hear it again.

'*They . . . found . . . the . . . bookman . . . dead . . . in . . . bed . . . this . . . morning*.' The speaker looked for a shock effect in the old man's expression but there was none. It came as an anti-climax. People began to fidget.

'What bookman?' Larry took a sip of his beer, licked his frothy lips.

The farmer looked heavenwards, closed his eyes and opened them again. 'The fellow they brought in to value the books. *Kroll's books*.'

'Oh, I see. Never heard of 'im, didn't know that anybody had come to value the books.'

'Larry, the guy has *died*.'

'Everybody has to die some time.' Larry winked, chuckling in his own peculiar way. 'Even me, but I'm not ready to go yet. Too much to do first.'

'Larry, he went into Kroll's house and the next morning he was dead. Like Mickey Farrell died because he threw an apple at him. And Joe Kinson, year before last, because he puked on Kroll's doorstep on his way home from the pub. Get it?'

'I don't get it at all.' Larry was maybe winding them all

up, took a delight in the way everybody crowded him. Secretly, he enjoyed being the centre of attraction. 'Kroll never hurt anybody, take it from me. Mean as a miser but he meant no harm.'

'How do *you* know, Larry?'

Larry took his time answering, a long drink and a swallow. 'Cause I did some work for him two, mebbe three, years ago. Can't be exactly certain how long. Tidied up the yard out back but I see it's as bad now, if not worse, than it was before. He was too mean to pay to have it done again.'

'You did *what*?'

'You heard, Joe, or are you goin' deaf?'

The gathering stepped back. Suddenly Larry wasn't the kind of guy you wanted to get too close to.

'*You* worked for *Kroll*?'

'Can't understand what all the fuss is about. Kroll never *hurt* nobody but you wouldn' a want him for your uncle. If he was your uncle –' Larry gave a smoker's laugh, rattled his lungs – 'you wouldn'a have much in the way of a Christmas box!'

'Kroll killed the bookman,' a hesitant voice said from the back of the throng.

'Poppycock!' Larry rounded on his stool, mocked them with his pale blue eyes. 'Kroll's dead. The dead never hurt nobody, it's the living you want to watch out for. You ask Victor, if you don't believe me, he's handled more corpses than he's had hot dinners and none ever did him no harm. What say you, Victor?'

Victor Pohl had gone several shades paler than his normal pallid complexion. 'Kroll's not normal, dead or alive.'

'He came back from the grave to murder the bookman!' The man at the back yelled.

'You'll be saying it's Dracula done it next.' Larry was clearly enjoying the exchange. 'All right, then, how'd this bookman fellow die?'

'Angina. So Dr King said,' a stout woman replied grudgingly.

'There you are, then.' Larry's voice was shrill, triumphant. 'Death from natural causes, as they say. You can't blame

Kroll for that, any more'n you can blame him for that kid running under a truck.'

'Kroll doesn't have to touch you to fucking kill you!' A sallow-faced young man yelled, his eyes blazing. 'He's some kind of devil, his body might've died but his spook's still around the town. You can fucking feel it!'

'Watch your language!' Larry sat bolt upright, shook a remonstrating finger.

'I'll fucking swear if I want to.'

'Landlord!' The old man looked round for Frank Minton, saw that the other was pulling a pint for a customer at the opposite end of the bar. 'Landlord, perhaps you'd care to do something about this filthy language.'

'It doesn't bother me,' Frank replied, clearly embarrassed.

'Well, it does *me*!' Larry rapped on the bar top with a coin. 'There's no need for that kind of dirty talk, I told Norma up at the Lion that it was time she had a word with one or two of her customers about their filthy talk.'

A silence descended on the bar room, folks glanced awkwardly at one another.

'Perhaps you can remember, Larry, when it was that Edward Kroll first moved into Knighton.' A large woman was not going to let him divert the subject of tonight's discussion. They all hated and feared Kroll but they wanted to talk about him. A kind of witch hunt.

'Don't rightly remember when Edward Kroll came here,' Larry answered as he refreshed himself from his glass, seemed to relax a little. 'But his father owned that house right back to the First World War, maybe before it.'

'His *father*?'

'That's right, so folks used to say. Never saw him myself, but the old fellers that came back from the war told me about him. Didn't live there all the time, used to come in the summer mostly. A kind of second house, I s'pose. So maybe Edward did the same, kept to himself like and the people never saw him, never knew he stayed there. Maybe he retired from whatever he did and decided to move here to live. I'd say he's been living here twenty years, could be more, could be less. But he's gone now. I'm not a churchgoer meself, but I reckon it's wrong to speak ill of the dead, particularly what you lot've been saying.'

'He killed the bookman, no doubt about that,' a sullen voice repeated.

'Aye.' A whispered agreement. 'Kroll's still here even though he's dead.'

'I went by the cemetery this morning,' the woman said, 'purposely. I wasn't going in there, but I looked over the wall and now that the leaves have fallen you can see right the way in. His grave was untouched so at least he hasn't got up out of it!'

'Stupid woman!' Larry finished his beer, drained his chaser. He got down from his stool like there was an urgency to get to the lavatory, but the way he folded his coat over his arm and tugged his cap down, told the regulars that he was finished here for the night.

'Off up to the Lion to listen to the filthy talk, Larry?' A jibe from the one whom Larry had reprimanded.

'Good night!' The crowd parted for him, all eyes watched him, his military-style walk, his haste.

'I think we've offended him,' Victor Pohl said through his cigarette.

Everybody laughed but it sounded forced.

Larry was not offended. In fact, he was chuckling to himself as he walked up Broad Street with a speed that made a mockery of his age. He had long mastered the art of winding-up the regulars in the George, it was a sport that he delighted in and they hadn't rumbled him after all these years!

'Worked for Kroll!' He spoke aloud, laughed again. 'I wouldn'a work for him because he wouldn'a pay you.' But it had been a good joke that had come spontaneously to his alert brain. All the same, there had been rumours years ago that a Kroll had owned that house and used it for holidays. True or false, Larry wasn't really interested. These folks were frightened of their own shadows. Kroll had killed the bookman? Poppycock and fiddlesticks!

Larry did not have his own stool in the Red Lion because his final call on Saturday nights was brief. A shandy to quench his thirst, a dry sherry to whet his appetite in readiness for his fish and chips supper. He was a man of routine that had spanned several decades and he had no plans to change it now.

'Good night, Larry,' Norma called after him as he departed with a speed that was comparable with that with which he had left the George and Dragon.

It was hunger that hurried him now for he relished his Saturday night supper.

A cod and a large portion of soggy fries, just the way he liked them, the greaseproof bag wrapped up in a newspaper to keep out the November cold night air. He tucked them under his arm, hurried down the steep Narrows. There wasn't anybody about, the locals still avoided this street, walked double the distance to the chippie.

What a lot of darned cowards! Larry cleared his throat, spat. Frightened of an old man, frightened of his house, and now they were frightened of his bloomin' ghost! That was Edward Kroll's house over there, his keen eyes noted the building a few doors up from the Grillhouse.

A light was showing in a second floor window.

Larry slowed his pace, looked up. Now that would have half the townsfolk running for cover if they saw it! But they wouldn't see it because they'd avoid this place like the blessed plague!

His flesh prickled slightly, he shrugged it off with a laugh, he didn't want to start getting spooked like the rest of the folks hereabouts. Silly blighters!

Upstairs a shadow crossed the curtain, was gone as quickly as it had come.

There was somebody up there, all right. Larry watched but the shadow did not return.

He hesitated. It could be somebody working late, sorting out Kroll's belongings, maybe a distant relative who had turned up. Even Edmonds, the solicitor.

Kroll killed the bookman.

Stuff and nonsense! Larry's snigger did not come quite so easily this time.

At the very worst that could be a burglar up there, a thief

helping himself to Kroll's books. Larry had never read a book in his life, he couldn't understand what people wanted them for, stories that were the product of somebody else's imagination. All lies, in fact, made up yarns.

His conscience twinged, maybe he should call the police. He decided against it; the Knighton office wasn't manned during the night hours, you had to ring through to Llandrindod Wells, wait whilst they radioed a patrol car. You could be hanging about for bloomin' hours. His fish and chips would go cold; he wasn't going to stand around eating them in the street like the drunks did when the pubs chucked them out, he preferred to savour his weekly treat in the comfort of his own home.

No, blow it, it was none of his business. If somebody was daft enough to want to pinch a few books, then good luck to 'em! In all probability, the books would never even be missed.

And another thing, as a clean living citizen, he needed to satisfy his conscience, he owed Kroll no favours. If everybody else was scared of the old skinflint, even after he was dead, then Larry most certainly was not.

Larry began to move off, was unable to resist one last look up at that window.

The light had gone off, the room was in darkness.

That settled it, then, whoever was in the house had, more than likely, finished whatever they were doing, either sorting or stealing. Calling the police would be a sheer waste of time.

Larry walked fast down the Narrows, was aware that his legs were a little shaky. That was most likely due to his age, most chaps over ninety were either dead or in a wheelchair, he'd done a lot better than most and he still had a good way to go.

Back in the living room of his tiny terraced cottage at the rear of the church, Larry threw some kindling on the glowing embers of the fire, sat down in front of it and unwrapped his supper. He always ate out of the paper, to have used a plate would have detracted from his Saturday night treat.

Strangely, the fish and chips didn't taste as good as they usually did, maybe Tommy at the chippie had had them keeping warm for too long, hadn't done a last fry.

Larry did not manage to finish them, his appetite seemed to have palled. Usually, he ate ravenously. He crumpled up the remains, threw them in the bin. His night out had been spoiled by a lot of silly nonsense. Next Saturday, if anybody started raking up all that rubbish again, they'd be on the receiving end of his sharp tongue!

He went upstairs to bed but tonight sleep seemed to elude him. His mind was too active, kept turning over everything that had been said in the bar of the George and Dragon and everything that he should have said in reply. What a load of old tripe!

Outside, the fog which had been forming on the mountains since dusk, began to creep slowly down into the town, swirling and thickening in the deserted streets.

As though there was something that needed to be hidden before the sleeping population awoke.

Part Two

After Death

Eleven

Each year the Grillhouse put on a pre-Christmas lunch in the run-up to the festive season: roast turkey with all the trimmings; a choice of either Christmas pudding or a dessert from the menu; coffee and a mince pie at the all-inclusive price of £4.25. Ginger's offered the same; The Clocktower Teashop competed with a vegetarian dinner, a nut roast and Golden Pudding. For the conventional seasonal diner the Grillhouse offering was possibly the best value for money. At least, the Morgans claimed that it was.

'We'll have to get in another half dozen turkeys,' John said as he brought through a tray of dirty crocks into the kitchen. 'Twenty-six Christmas dinners so far today. That must be the record. Last year we did twenty on Christmas Eve but I don't reckon we'll better today.'

'It's barely half past one yet.' Christine turned to look at the clock on the Belling. 'Bet you there'll be one or two stragglers.'

'Could be,' he said as he began to fill the dishwasher, 'though generally we don't do much after half one. Still, it'll make a difference to our Christmas.'

'You can say that again,' she agreed with a laugh. 'If we can have a good Christmas I don't mind struggling through for the rest of the year.'

'Rick can have his air rifle now.'

'No, John, *please*, not an airgun.'

'We can't deny him, darling. Every boy goes through the airgun phase. I had one.'

'Yes, but . . .' She dried her hands on the towel just a bit too vigorously. 'You know Rick. Next thing we'll have the police round because there's been a street lamp smashed and the vet's treated a cat for a pellet wound. Just like happened when he had that catapult for his birthday two years ago.'

'That was two years ago.'

'And he hasn't changed any.'

'He's stayed in a lot lately.'

'Agreed, but that's because of . . .' She left the sentence unfinished. A lot of folks had stayed home these last few weeks, more so since that book dealer had been found dead in bed at the Red Lion. 'Anyway, we can discuss it later.'

'Folks are walking up and down the Narrows again now.' He attempted to reassure her.

'A few.'

'Things will change. Slowly, I guess. Once *his* house is sold and somebody *normal* moves in to live there, people will forget.'

'Nobody will ever forget, John. You know that.'

He sighed, Chrissie was right, as usual. But, at least, maybe there would be a semblance of a normal community on the surface. 'The school breaks up tomorrow.'

'I haven't forgotten—' she made an attempt at a smile – 'but Rick and Tom will have Christmas to take their minds off things. It's afterwards that worries me. You know, that sort of anti-climax feeling and we always get bad weather in January. A foot of snow gives me a kind of . . . trapped feeling. John . . .'

'Yes?'

'I've been thinking . . . well, we'll have to discuss it later but . . . there are dozens of other places besides Knighton where we could run a successful restaurant.'

'I guessed you were thinking along those lines,' he said.

'Were you?'

'It had occurred to me but it wouldn't be right for the boys just now. Better to let them finish school and then look for somewhere. Maybe the Midlands, they'd stand a better chance of finding a job over there.'

'Maybe, it would mean staying on here another couple of years. Anyway, it's something we can be thinking about.'

The bell on the street door clanged.

'You've got another customer.'

'How many Christmas dinners left?'

'I can go to two, stretch it to three at a pinch.'

'I'll see what they want. Bet you it's only a coffee and a mince pie.'

'I'll have to bake some more of those, too. We're on the last tray in the freezer.' She heard him going through to the dining area.

John Morgan scarcely glanced at the man with his back towards him who was preparing to sit down at the corner table. A thought crossed his mind that the man could just as easily have seated himself at one of the tables which had already been cleared and wiped over. Instead, the stranger was agitatedly, clumsily, lining up dirty cups and saucers and side plates on the opposite side, muttering his annoyance to himself.

A stranger, but even from the rear there was something disturbingly familiar about him, the trilby hat, the frayed coat . . . John's stomach balled, his heartbeat stepped up a gear. No, it was his imagination playing cruel tricks with him; there were dozens of men of pensionable age in this town who dressed like that, widowers who had developed their own quirks in the twilight of their lives. Senility came in gradual stages, many muttered to themselves, even carried on a conversation. Like this one was doing right now. Just another bad-tempered, lonely old man.

'I'll clear that table for you, sir, in just one moment. Or, if you prefer, there's a couple of vacant ones already laid over here.'

The man might not have heard him; saucers and plates were being stacked on top of one another, used knives and teaspoons laid side by side, all the same way up, edge to edge, being straightened where they were out of alignment.

Oh, my God, no! It's impossible!

The chair was pulled back, real or imaginary crumbs dusted off with a hand. Thin shoulders hunched, the frail body stooped, he wiped an area of the window free of condensation so that it could be used as a mirror. The hat was adjusted but not removed. Then, slowly, the emaciated figure turned round.

John Morgan would have screamed had not his vocal chords suddenly ceased to function. Instead, he mimed a shocked cry; he might have turned and fled back into the kitchen but for the fact that his legs had become weak and trembled. He heard his jotter flutter from his fingers like a dying butterfly, thud on the carpet. His vision blurred, distorted the awful countenance that was turned upon him.

The gyrating room steadied, his vision cruelly cleared and assured him that there was no mistake.

Edward Kroll had returned.

He sat down, shuffled the chair back and forth until it was positioned to his satisfaction. The seemingly fleshless hands were rubbed together, the thin lips pouted. 'This table is a disgrace, littered with dirty crockery, scattered with crumbs.'

'I'll . . . I'll clean it off at once.'

'Please do so. In the meantime . . .' He bent forward, squinted at the menu, his dark eyes seemed to glaze over as if he was blind. 'Today is Thursday, is it not?'

'Yes.' John Morgan had lost all track of time, his brain was numbed. It was easier to answer in the affirmative than to try to think.

'I thought it was. Just lately I've become disoriented.'

John's flesh went icy cold, he got a feeling that the hair on his head might have been trying to stand upright.

'Cottage pie, chips and peas with a slice of buttered bread.'

'I'll get it right away.' He turned, felt himself lurch, grabbed at a chair to steady himself.

'*Wait*!'

It was as if one of the man's thin arms had shot out, grasped him with ice cold fingers, stayed him by force.

'I've been ill in bed for quite a time, out of touch. How long is it until Christmas?'

'Er . . . about a week, just over, I think.'

'I hate Christmas, always have, even as a boy. I always resisted the temptation to fritter away money. But I think, on this occasion, I shall break my Thursday routine and partake of your pre-Christmas fare even though it is a pound dearer than the cottage pie. Possibly, as a regular customer, even though I have been absent for a time, your generosity might prevail and afford me a small reduction. Say, four pounds?'

'Yes, yes, I'm sure we can do that.'

'And an ample enough portion to provide me with some supper, doubtless.' The Tupperware box, scratched and grimed, appeared on the table, was straightened so that it lay in a direct line with the edge. 'First, though, this table requires cleaning.'

Christine was over by the window that looked out on to the yard, slumped against the wide sill, her head in her hands, her body shaking uncontrollably. John stood there just inside the doorway, he could not think of anything to say. She had overheard, there was nothing else to add.

She turned around slowly, peered through her fingers as though she was afraid of what she might see. 'John.' A hoarse, frightened whisper. 'It's . . . impossible.'

'Evidently not.' He had to play it down for Chrissie's sake, there *had* to be a plausible explanation. Right now he had to come up with his best guess. 'He's been ill. In bed. He's better now.'

'John . . .' A frightened gasp, her voice was lowered until it was scarcely audible. 'They . . . they buried him!'

'Some kind of a mistake, don't ask me what right now. Maybe it was somebody else who died, they got mixed up. Yes, that's it, that's what must've happened.' It'll do for now, you've just got to believe it in order to keep your sanity, he told himself.

'I . . . I don't want him in here, John!'

'At the moment we don't have any choice. I'll go clean the table off to keep him happy, you get a dinner ready. We'll talk about it later, OK?'

It wasn't OK but there was no alternative. He grabbed up a cloth, was on his way back into the dining room when the outer doorbell chimed again. John Morgan paused, watched.

It was Aggie and Barbara, they had been in yesterday, they were returning to their old haunt, it seemed.

'We'll sit over in the corner, Ag.'

'All right, even if *'e* used to perch there. God, it's bloody cold in 'ere, cuttin' back on the heating to pay for Christmas, I s'pose.'

Aggie let out a scream, a shrill shriek that was deafening in the confined space, staggered back and trod on her companion's foot.

Then Barbara was screaming, too, and not because of the pain in her toes. Both women stared, their features drained of colour as they clutched at each other.

'*No*!' This time the shriek was in unison. They backed away.

The object of their terror appeared to be oblivious of their presence, he was studying the menu intensely, making mental calculations with the aid of his skeletal fingers, holding a muttered conversation with himself, evidently doubting his own arithmetical capabilities.

The two women bumped into each other as they turned, nearly overbalanced, then fled for the exit. Out into the street, shoppers stared in amazement at two elderly women fleeing down the Narrows, screaming incoherently.

The open Grillhouse door swung gently on its hinges, buffeted by an icy mountain breeze, creaking and groaning its protest.

'*Door*!' Kroll's cadaverous features were a mask of fury, his roar of rage seemed to vibrate the restaurant then rushed out into the street, echoing its way down towards the clock-tower.

His gaze returned to the menu, he clucked his irritation at having lost count on his bony digits.

John walked across and closed the door quietly, jangling the bell again. The sweat on his body had gone cold. Jesus, this was disastrous, neither Aggie nor Barbara would ever set foot in here again. Word would spread, Kroll's shout had doubtless been heard all the way down into town, the inhabitants would know that their worst nightmare had been realized, that Edward Kroll had returned from his grave.

Kroll ate ravenously in his own peculiar and revolting way, cutting the sliced turkey into minute pieces, chewing fast and furiously, appearing to make no impression upon his heaped plate. Particles of skin or gristle were spat out amidst a dribble of gravy, carefully and systematically displayed on the edge of his plate. He belched loudly at frequent intervals, lifted a wasted buttock off his chair to break wind.

After a while, he paused, began to segregate his supper from his lunch; slices of carrot, peas and sprouts were carefully counted into their respective equal halves; once he lost his tally, began all over again.

He's mad and I'm going bloody mad, too. John was an hypnotic spectator from the kitchen doorway. Christine had fled upstairs, maybe he ought to have gone up to comfort her.

Outside, the Narrows was deserted. Already the townspeople were deserting it. By tomorrow it would be a ghost street.

'*Finished*!'

John jumped, almost ran to take the empty plate, saw how the gravy had been mopped up with the bread roll. Only the much masticated rejected particles remained.

'*Pudding*!'

A chilling command that had to be obeyed, a screech that was scarcely human. John sensed that Kroll had changed; previously he had just been unpleasant, sinister because the townspeople had built up that image.

Now he was evil.

John brought the bowl of Christmas pudding through, watched how the other halved it, together with the mince pie, slurped his coffee noisily and placed the saucer on top of the cup to keep the brew from cooling. It was already after three o'clock, today Kroll was breaking his strict routine. His visit was clearly going to be a lengthy one.

Kroll spooned at the custard, gave an exclamation of annoyance and pain, spat and sprayed thick yellow droplets across the table. 'It's boiling!'

'Of course, it's come straight out of the oven.'

'You should have warned me!' A glare, the spoon was stabbed accusingly.

'I'm sorry, Mr Kroll.' John felt physically sick. And scared like he'd never been before.

The other bent forward, lips pouted, and began blowing over his spoon, the spoon waving in time with each gust. He wiped his lips with a serviette, grabbed for his coffee again. 'Ugh! Bitter!'

'It's a fresh brew.'

Kroll tore at a sachet of sugar, shook it. Some of the grains spilled across the table. Another three sweetners followed the first, then he was stirring as if right now it was the most important task in the world.

'I'll have to wait for the pudding to cool.' Impatiently he reached across for a newspaper which one of the diners had left on the next table. Oblivious of the custard droplets, he spread it out, produced a small magnifying glass from his pocket, bent forward, squinted.

'Will there be anything else, Mr Kroll?' John's instinct was to be away from this nauseating creature who was supposed to be lying in his grave in the cemetery. There had to be some explanation for the man's return but right now he couldn't think of one that would quell his rising terror and revulsion.

'The table needs wiping.' He lifted the newspaper, it peeled stickily out of the splashed, congealing custard. 'And I'll take my mince pie home with me.'

'I won't be a moment.' John turned away, his walk was erratic, it seemed impossible to maintain a straight course for the kitchen doorway. Thank God Christine had gone upstairs and the boys were at school. He was panicking, he couldn't remember where the cloths were kept, opening cutlery drawers and crockery cupboards, a confused search that finally led him to the cleaning utensils beneath the sink.

'*Cloth*!'

The cry was bloodchilling, like a vampire screeching its lust into the night. John stumbled, almost fell, staggering back into the dining area where Edward Kroll was holding his newspaper aloft with a strained expression on his face as though the pages weighed heavy.

John's fingers trembled, the glazed surface smeared as he wiped, crumbs showered on to the floor.

'I shall take this newspaper home with me.' Kroll laid it flat, attempting to press the creases as he shuffled the pages evenly. 'I can never understand how anybody can read a creased and crumpled paper!' He banged on it with a puny fist. 'It detracts from the contents.'

'Er, no, neither can I.' John's voice quavered, he would agree with anything that the man said right now. A fearful glance at his customer, the other did not appear any different from his last visit. *Nothing* had changed.

And that made it a thousand times more frightening.

Kroll slurped at his custard again, appeared to be chewing it, his mouth moving rapidly in what could only be an appreciation of the delicate flavour. A tiny portion of Christmas pudding was lifted up, examined. A discerning mastication was followed by the spitting out of a particle of fruit. It landed on the table, he did not seem to notice.

'If that's all, Mr Kroll, I have some chores to be doing up in the kitchen.'

A wave of his spoon signified that permission to leave was granted. Kroll did not look up, something in one of the printed columns required a closer examination through the lens, he bent forward until his hooked nose touched the handle of his glass.

John Morgan returned to the kitchen, stood there silently shaking. It was impossible to concentrate on any of the jobs that awaited him; the surface tops needed cleaning, the dishwasher switched off, waited to be emptied, a bag of garbage needed to be put outside. He was totally disoriented.

An awful silence had descended upon the Grillhouse, broken only by Edward Kroll's noisy eating, interspersed with unintelligible mutterings. From upstairs came the sound of sobbing, Christine was reacting in the only way she knew how.

At a quarter to four, John heard the clock on the tower down the street give a trio of chimes, the outer door banged. The grisly customer had finished his messy meal and departed, returned to his awful abode of cold dampness that stank of death.

That realization in itself was bad enough, John clutched at the worktop to steady himself. Worse was the knowledge that this ogre of the small town and its surrounding mountains was back, had somehow survived the funeral rites and the burial, would walk amongst them again. And, John almost screamed aloud at the awful thought, the other would continue to obtain the sustenance required by his emaciated body in this very restaurant.

Twelve

'Jesus Christ is risen!' Only Dr King's sardonic smile betrayed his scepticism. 'Except that I'm fairly certain that whatever the shape or form of the Second Coming it won't be in the guise of Edward Kroll! Our friend is in no way the product of a virgin birth, more likely he was discovered beneath a stone!'

PC Phil Morris shuddered at the allusion to some cold, slimy reptilian creature. 'I have to agree with you there, doc.'

'So, what's the problem?' Mervyn King invited the policeman to voice it in the words of the scared inhabitants of Knighton for there was no way he wanted to be quoted on wild supposition fuelled by superstition.

The constable glanced nervously from the doctor to Edmonds. The three of them were seated in the lawyer's office; the latter was looking for both a medical and a police opinion. Down below, with the approach of dusk, the street was deserted. Far better had Kroll not died than *this* to have happened. All three of them were in a no-win situation.

'Well?'

Phil cleared his throat, scarcely trusting himself to speak. 'As we all know. Kroll is back. You certified him dead, doc.' He dropped his eyes, it sounded like an accusation.

'I did!' The reply was abrupt, chillingly confident. 'Because he *was* dead. I didn't order a PM, there was no need. He died of heart failure brought about by bronchial pneumonia, the commonest cause of death amongst the over-seventies in winter. So, where do we go from there?'

'He . . . he hasn't altered any, he's just the same as he was before. He ate in the Grillhouse today, one of their pre-Christmas dinners, scoffed half and kept the rest for his supper like he always does. Naturally, folks are saying that he's risen from the grave and can you blame them? There's only one alternative, that he wasn't dead in the first place, that it was all a mistake . . .'

'I told you, I examined him and wrote out a death certificate on the strength of my findings!' Dr King was angry, he did not tolerate fools and the police officer was questioning his professional ability. 'There *is* another alternative but, quite obviously, you haven't thought that far yet!'

The policeman looked to the lawyer; the doctor had pushed them both into a corner. As usual, the alert brain of the ageing medic was one step ahead of them.

'Do tell us, please,' Edmonds said as he leaned back in his chair, closing his eyes, all part of a repartee which he had enjoyed with his friend over the years. 'I'm intrigued. A reincarnation, but in the same person as before?'

'I would dare to suggest –' King's expression was stoic – 'and I seldom presume anything, that Edward Kroll had an identical twin brother, a recluse like himself. Upon hearing of his brother's death, Kroll Two decided to continue where Kroll One left off, and has just moved into Knighton. As the next of, and again presumably, the only kin, he has every right to do so. Pending probate, naturally. Doubtless, there are formalities, procedures which must be followed in order to satisfy the collector of taxes, George. I know nothing of such matters, I am merely a general practitioner. But, the way I see it, it is hardly a police matter, is it?'

'How do we prove it?' There was no disguising the relief on Phil's face at the possibility of a plausible explanation; when the dead walked you clutched at any available straw. The doctor's theory *had* to be the right one because no God-fearing citizen would accept the only other possibility.

'As Phil says, we have to *prove* it.' His hand shook just a little as he lit a cigarette.

'Well, the ball's in your court . . .' For a moment the others thought that King might heave himself up out of his chair and leave, he was that kind of man. They had his input, he was not one to discuss other wild possibilities. 'An exhumation?'

'Not easy,' Edmonds grunted, drew deeply on his cigarette, shook his head. 'The Home Office would want more proof than just local scared gossip. First, they would demand that the occupant of Kroll's house was thoroughly investigated. You can't go just digging bodies up to see if they're in order. Even if an exhumation was authorized, the paperwork takes weeks except in the case of a major police enquiry.' He smiled at the constable. 'Over to you, Phil.'

'*We'd* better have a chat to Kroll himself, or whoever he is.' The emphasis was on the 'we', he wasn't going alone this time. Sergeant Davison would find some excuse for dodging the visit, pass the proverbial buck.

'On what grounds?' Edmonds raised his eyebrows. 'No felony has been committed. Excuse us, Mr Kroll, but we think you're dead and we have a certificate to prove it. We might have made a mistake, though, so if you would enlighten us, we'd appreciate it. Next thing we know, he's written to the Police Complaints Board and lodged a complaint for harassment.'

'We have to check in case you're an impostor,' Phil Morris countered. 'We have the deceased's . . . er, pardon me, *your* legacy to protect. We're only acting in your interests.'

Edmonds grimaced. 'Sounds weak but I guess it'll have to do. And if you can't prove your identity, Mr Kroll, would you mind the doc checking you over?'

'Thanks a million for dropping me in the shit!' King puffed out his cheeks. 'He won't agree to that, I'll promise you. Anyway, I'll come along, just to be sociable. Drinks all round and a laugh thrown in for good measure!'

'Well, when do we go, then?' Phil was relieved at the prospect of company. The telephone at the police station had been ringing non-stop since three forty-five. Just like the time a few years back when that author guy had given his fans a spoof 'midnight vampire walk' and scared some of the residents. Now the entire population was terrified and on this occasion he could not blame them. Their bogeyman had to be laid to rest once and for all but he had an uneasy premonition that it wouldn't work out quite like that.

* * *

There was a light showing in one of the upper windows of Kroll's house, even as they watched a shadow fell across it; a silhouetted, trilby-hatted hunched shape. The watchers' mouths went dry but at least they had not come on a fool's errand.

Phil tried to make his knock sound authoritative; this time it did not echo, just a dull thumping as if the interior of the dark house was rejecting it.

The light upstairs went out, the place was plunged into impenetrable blackness.

Suddenly the door was open and Edward Kroll stood there on the step, framed by the dim passageway light behind him. No rattling of a lock, no scraping of a warped door on a worn stone floor. A silent appearance that had all three men stepping back, bumping into one another in their shocked surprise

'I was in bed, you disturbed me.' A nightshirt fell below the knee-length topcoat, trailed on the floor. The features were in deep shadow but if you could not see them, you knew only too well that the mouth was twisted into an angry snarl, that the deep-sunken eyes watched you balefully. 'I am recuperating from a severe attack of influenza. Could your visit not have waited until a more reasonable hour?'

The town clock struck six as if to emphasize the speaker's aggrieved words. For a moment the trio were on the verge of offering an apology and retiring.

'We'd like to talk to you, Mr Kroll.' Edmonds stepped forward. 'It's important, in *your* interests.'

Kroll was silent, this time his expression was impossible to guess.

Phil was aware that he fidgeted uneasily, hoped that the others didn't notice. He experienced a sense of inferiority that bordered on humility. Dr King gave a slight smoker's cough, it surely was not a nervous hack.

They waited.

'Come inside, please.' The whisper was a frightening anti-climax to their expectations. Kroll turned, they saw him shuffling back down the bookstacked corridor, leaving them to follow. 'And don't forget to close the door behind you.'

It was cold and crowded in the small kitchen, the stench of mustiness was overpowering. The table was the same as it had been before, a neat array of unopened preserves and stacked coins, the empty chairs did not look inviting.

'Well?' The wasted features were impassive, the question one that any householder might have asked of an unsolicited deputation.

'There's a problem', Edmonds was the spokesman again, he seemed to have regained his composure.

'A *problem*?'

'Yes, yes.' The lawyer swallowed. 'But I'm sure it can be resolved quite easily. You see . . .' His voice tailed off.

'No, I don't see at all!'

It was as though the temperature in that unheated room had suddenly dropped several degrees.

'There was a death, a funeral . . . quite recently.'

'Oh! Whose, and what has it got to do with me?'

'The deceased –' George Edmonds fidgeted with a cigarette pack in his pocket, his craving for tobacco had never been stronger than it was this very minute – 'was one . . . Edward Kroll.'

'This is preposterous.' The man stiffened, his head was thrust forward, the others smelled his fetid breath, turned their heads.

'So it seems, but there is a death certificate . . .'

'*Show it to me*!'

Edmonds winced visibly. 'At the moment the copy is with the local registrar of births and deaths. The original has been sent to the General Register Office.' Shit, they should have brought it with them.

'Obviously a gross mistake, then, don't you agree?'

'Possibly, but we have to confirm that it's a mistake for the reassurance of . . .' He almost said "the townsfolk' but checked himself just in time. 'The Commissioners of Oaths and the Collector of Taxes. I would hate you to receive a bill for inheritance tax, Mr Kroll.'

'I should rip it up.'

'Understandably so. But we were hoping that the mistake could be rectified without having to resort to official channels.'

'How?'

Jesus Christ, this was it! George Edmonds took a deep breath, glanced briefly at his companions. 'If you would agree to allow Dr King to examine you . . .'

'What on earth for?'

'Just to . . . to make sure that you are . . . all right.'

Kroll's intake of breath was a long drawn-out hiss.

'Or to ensure that I am not dead?'

Phil Morris recoiled as though he had received a physical blow, he almost clutched at Dr King. The cold was intense, arctic; the stench like that of some wild animal's lair. For Jesus Christ's sake, let's get the hell out of here!

'If you put it that way, yes.' George Edmonds spoke with unbelievable casualness. 'It might satisfy everybody concerned without time-wasting procedures.'

The dusty light bulb flickered, steadied. Breath vapourized.

'Very well, but it will have to be brief. Let's get it over and done with, doctor, then I can return to bed.'

Dr King stared in disbelief, never in his wildest dreams had he expected the other to agree to an examination. 'Well, that's fine . . .' A sudden thought that brought a muttered 'fuck it' to his lips. In the confusion he had forgotten to bring his medical bag with him!

'OK, doc?' Edmonds sensed by his companion's hesitation that there was some kind of hitch.

'Fine.' The medic was a past master at overcoming a blunder. 'Just a quick check will be all that is necessary, Mr Kroll. I'd like to take your pulse first.'

The pulse revealed a lot, blood pressure equipment was merely a more detailed confirmation of early findings. Mervyn King stepped forward, noticed how his companions backed away and not just to make room for him.

'Now, if I could just have your wrist . . .'

A hand was held out, the sleeve hanging from the wrist like an oversize drape; rock steady, not so much as a tremor. Even in the dim light from the low wattage bulb the skin appeared translucent, a skeleton with a stretched polythene covering. King took a deep breath, inhaled an unpleasant odour.

Like the body in front of him was decomposing.

He winced, contact was icy, transmitted a goosebumping to his own flesh. He braced himself, felt around the wrist; pulses were sometimes difficult to locate.

He thought he found what he was searching for, could not be absolutely certain because his own fingers were trembling, numbing fast. It was colder in here than in Victor Pohl's mortuary and smelled much the same.

Ah, that *had* to be it! The tremor was so faint that the doctor could not be absolutely certain. It was akin to the pulse of a badly injured road accident victim, barely perceptible and fading rapidly.

King's first reaction was that his patient was dying. As if to contradict him, Kroll let out a blast of lower wind, breathed in deeply, there was a sense of satisfaction in his inhalation. His impassive expression did not alter, there was not so much as a flickering of his eyelids.

'Pulse is OK.' The doctor's proclamation lacked his usual conviction.

The other did not answer, stood there staring straight ahead of him. King wished that he had a thermometer, he had never experienced a patient, even in the final stages of a terminal illness, whose flesh was so cold.

'Just a look at your eyes, please.' Politeness was not one of the doctor's attributes, it came with a feeling of awe. This was an impossible situation, a nightmarish joke played by students at medical college, they had dressed up a corpse, wired it to a battery or something that gave the impression of life within death. It couldn't be real. It was.

Those deep-set orbs were like volcanic fires deep in a crater, you felt their heat and backed off. You were scared to look.

'Hmm . . .' This could be interpreted in innumerable ways. 'Open your mouth . . . please.'

Jesus on Sunday! The stench was foul, vaporized in the cold atmosphere as though to screen whatever lay within that awesome cavity. King glimpsed blackened and rotting teeth, the tongue was heavily furred but he wasn't going to investigate any further. He jerked his head away, wanted to retch.

'I would advise a visit to a dentist, Mr Kroll.'

'I never suffer from toothache.'

That was probably true, the teeth had rotted, the nerves were long dead.

Strong or weak, the heart was functioning; it had to be or else Kroll would not be breathing and breaking wind. That was logical; King ducked the formality of requesting the other to unbutton his coat. Perhaps, with the aid of a stethoscope, he might have listened from afar but no way was he putting his ear up against *that*.

'Anything else, doctor?'

'Your bronchitis appears to have improved since we last met, Mr Kroll.' That was uncanny, indeed, the man's frailty, the lack of heating in the house, should have hastened pneumonia. Those lungs were no longer rattling and rasping. The nostrils were not clogged with mucus. A dribble strung from the lips but the saliva was clear.

'Just the occasional touch of phlegm first thing in the morning, it doesn't trouble me once I've coughed it up.'

'Quite.' Dr King looked round at his companions, both the policeman and the lawyer showed signs of feeling sick. 'You smoke?'

'One cigarette a day, consumed in three sessions, morning, noon and evening.'

'I see. You appear to be in reasonable health for your age, Mr Kroll, which is . . .?'

'It should be on your records. This death certificate, you mentioned, the case of mistaken identity, it will surely be on that.'

'It must be, we'll have to check it, anyway.' It wasn't because the surgery receptionist was still trying to locate Edward Kroll's medical record sheet. King had hazarded a guess when he had scribbled out the death certificate; he could not remember what he had written. 'It's immaterial right now.'

'Is that all, doctor?'

'I guess so.'

'In which case I trust that you will not trouble me again. As you can see, I am alive and well, and this nonsense over my supposed death is all a mistake. I trust you will rectify it for the records . . . when you find them!'

'I'll see to it.'

The trio had a feeling of being herded back down the passageway towards the front door, an ageing shepherd driving his humble flock before him, a master in control of lesser creatures.

The door was slammed after them, they heard the key grating in the lock, a bolt being shot home. Then they were huddling together in the street, three men whose roles in life had fitted them for dealing with death in its every form.

Death, they could have accepted. Life, as they had just witnessed it, was too terrible to contemplate if they wished to retain their sanity.

Thirteen

Charles Chadwick had an annoying habit of whistling tunelessly when he was deep in thought. Mostly he had no idea that he was doing it. Like today.

He always watched football on television on Sunday afternoons, it was a kind of religion with him in much the same way that others went to chapel or church. In his mind he lived what might have been his true life had not a serious knee injury robbed him of a promising sporting career at twenty. Ten years on, he was envious of every player who wore a number 7 shirt, lived every moment of every match he watched as if it was himself out there on the pitch; his deformed leg fidgeted and twitched, felt the impact of every tackle, every kick. Reporting on games for a local newspaper was no substitute for stardom.

But today, although he stared at the television screen, his expression was blank; he clasped and unclasped his hands, entwined his fingers, clenched his fists. And his lips were pouted, emitting a series of low whistles.

Lindy Lloyd, his lover these past five years since Chad had parted from his wife, stood in the living room doorway watching him. Clearly he had something on his mind, a dilemma, some problem that he was trying to sort out and it had to be an important one to distract him from his beloved game.

'If you're not bothered with the match, switch the telly off, please, Chad.' She came into the room, handed him a mug of coffee. 'You know how I hate football.'

'I'm watching it.' He saw that the bathrobe she wore was only loosely belted, showing him a glimpse of her slim nakedness. Her fair hair was bedraggled, she had obviously just got out of the bath. Maybe she had other things in mind, right now even sex didn't interest him. He turned back to the screen.

'No, you're not, you're preoccupied with something else, I can tell.' She didn't like the way he had taken to tying his hair back in a ponytail, preferring it to hang loose around the neck of his Aston Villa sweatshirt. He had put on a little weight lately; not a lot, maybe ten pounds. In fact, right now she was looking for every fault she could find with him because he was in one of his annoying moods. All he ever thought about was football, either watching it on television or going to local matches and spending the evenings writing up his reports. It wasn't football on his mind, that was for sure, or else he would have been kicking imaginary balls, shouting like he was there in person. It was something else, she groaned inwardly. She had always come a poor second to his football; now, apparently, something else was preoccupying him. She was damned if she was going to be relegated to third in his priorities.

The game had stopped, the players were walking off the field.

'Half-time!' he announced, just in case she thought the game was over.

'Great! So I've got to put up with another three-quarters of an hour!'

'Has it stopped snowing yet?' He seemed to shake himself out of a trance, looked up and smiled.

'Yes.' Her tone was abrupt, she wasn't fooled by his sudden change of attitude. 'Just a light covering on the ground outside but it'll probably freeze tonight and everywhere will be like a skating rink.' Just in case you're thinking of going out somewhere, like down to the pub to talk football all night with your buddies.

'It won't come to much, the worst of the weather always comes after Christmas. You wait and see if I'm not right, there'll be a foot of snow lying on New Year's Day.'

'You're obviously planning to go out tonight.' She moved across to the window of the flat they shared and looked down on to Knighton's main street. A gritting truck was coming slowly down from the direction of the clocktower. Otherwise, everywhere was deserted, just as it always was on Sundays.

'Perhaps.'

'Which means "yes". So I'll be on my own again which, I suppose, is no different from sitting here whilst you watch a re-run of the football all over again. At least I'll be able to watch what *I* want to. I just hope there's something decent on the box for a change.' She could not control her bitterness, life cooped up in a small flat with somebody whose interests were something you abhorred, was far from easy. They were getting on each other's nerves a lot lately.

They lapsed into silence, the way they always did when they had a difference of opinion. They seldom argued or rowed, perhaps it would be better if they did. Today would follow form, an awkward atmosphere, monosyllabic questions and answers, and then only when absolutely necessary.

Maybe Chad had got another woman. The idea alone brought with it a feeling of panic. No! No, it wasn't that, she would have known before now if he'd been having an affair. Her intuition would have told her. What, then?

'Something's bugging you, Chad. Either tell me, or don't. Please yourself.'

'I tried to get an interview yesterday. The Knighton game was called off at the last minute, the referee ruled that the ground was too hard after Friday night's frost. I had time on my hands, I also had an idea.'

'Tell me something new, you're full of ideas that don't work out, Chad. You phoned some big-name player, tried to arrange an interview and he told you to piss off.'

'Very funny, I don't think.' He turned back to the television, leaned forward, chin in cupped hands, tried to absorb himself in an advert.

'I'm sorry, Chad. It's being cooped up in this rabbit hutch that is making us get on each other's nerves. Tell you what, wherever you're going tonight, let me come with you. Maybe we could share it just for once.'

'Not this time.' It was the anxious tone in his voice that worried her.

'Why not? Where are you planning on going?'

'I tried to interview Edward Kroll yesterday,' he said in a hushed whisper as if he feared lest he might be overheard.

'Jesus! Are you crazy, Chad?'

'No. At least, I don't think so. I get the feeling there's some big cover-up. There *has* to be, logically. A guy can't die and be buried and then turn up and resume life as before. I don't believe in zombies, or the undead, or stuff like that. Everybody's dodging the issue. Apparently, this town is prepared to skulk behind closed doors and let everything go on as it always has. Trump, the features editor, refuses to write anything at all, says we might be sued for libel. But I reckon that one of the national tabloids might jump at the story. I can see the headlines, "Back from the Dead". Or something like that.'

'Why don't you give them a call, then?'

'You have to be kidding! Thanks for the tip-off, Chad, here's a hundred pounds to treat yourself with. I'd get the sack from the *Star* into the bargain, unethical reporting, breach of contract. Lindy, darling –' his hand found hers, squeezed it – 'please credit me for being born with more brains than that.'

'So you decided to try an interview off your own bat, write the feature and maybe syndicate it. Make a killing and fuck the *Star*. Sounds good but I get the impression that it didn't work out the way you planned. Kroll told you to sod off, end of story.'

'No, he didn't.'

'What'd he say, then, come back tomorrow night and I'll give you a complete run-down on life in the grave and after?'

'He wasn't home. At least, if he was, he didn't answer the door.'

'Oh, I see.'

'I tried talking to the Morgans at the Grillhouse, Kroll eats there Tuesdays and Thursdays. They wouldn't play ball, they're as scared of him as everybody else. It's a lone wolf game, that's for certain.'

'So . . .' She hesitated. 'You plan to go knocking on Kroll's door this evening. If he didn't answer yesterday afternoon, he probably won't tonight. So, you're wasting your time.' I don't want you to go up *there*. She was suddenly edgy.

'They found him dead in the house last time, didn't they?'

'What . . . what are you talking about, Chad?'

'He might be dead in there again!'

'*No*!'

'He's old and feeble at best. A guy could walk in and out of that hovel and he'd never know they'd been there. Of course, I'd knock first, make sure he's not up and about. I mean, the last time they went in there it was because he wasn't answering the door. Right?'

'Yes, but that was the police. And Dr King went, too.'

'Sure, but I'm the public spirited sort, not like these wimps who walk on by when somebody's getting raped or murdered, pretend they never saw anything wrong. I went up to call on Kroll to interview him, and when I got no response to my knocking, I thought I'd better just check.'

'You're crazier than I thought. Why don't you just stick to football reporting?'

'I can always go back to that, maybe get a job with one of the biggies, cover premier league matches.' The second half of the televised match was in progress but Chad seemed oblivious of it. There was a near-fanatical gleam in his eyes. 'You can come along if you really want, keep a lookout in the street for me.'

'No, *thank you*!' She shivered but it was not wholly at the thought of standing out in the freezing Narrows. 'You go if you want, there's no way I can stop you.'

Chad sat back with that same vacant expression on his rugged features. And when he began to whistle tunelessly again, Lindy knew without any doubt that he would go up to Edward Kroll's house later.

'Hello, Mr Edmonds, what can I do for you?' The attractive dark-haired girl looked up from her desk in the local office of the Registrar of Births and Deaths. I think we might be in for some snow over the weekend?'

'Morning, Daphne,' the lawyer replied as he rubbed his hands together, 'you could be right, the sky over Panpunton looks heavy with it. Sorry to bother you on a Saturday morning.'

'That's all right, that's what I'm here for, Saturdays are favourite for weddings, not that there's any today.'

'You remember Kroll's death certificate?'

She tensed instantly. 'Well, more or less. I sent it off to the GRO like I do every one.'

'They appear to have lost it.'

'I most certainly posted it.' Just in case you're trying to blame me. Let's all pass the buck. 'It could have got lost in the mail.'

'Possible, but not probable.' He tried to smile reassuringly. 'Everybody blames the mail, especially for losing cheques. Don't worry, I'm certain you mailed it.'

'If there's anything you want to check on, I can always get the copy out for you.'

'That's what I was hoping you'd say, I need to check on the details.'

'Take a seat, it might take me a few minutes but with any luck I'll put my hand straight on it.'

He seated himself in the rickety wicker chair, watched her go through to the adjacent filing room. There was a 'no smoking' sign on the desk but he knew Daphne wouldn't object, he could smell that she had been sneaking a smoke herself, probably stubbed it out hastily when she had heard him opening the door. He needed tobacco, suddenly he had gone tense.

He caught a faint rustling of papers from behind the closed door, envisaged her flipping through piles of banded certificates the way a bank cashier counted notes. He didn't have to listen so intently; he didn't have to stay, he could have called back later.

A sudden silence had his pulses racing. Then he heard her flicking on again. Damn it, he shouldn't be getting edgy this way. She muttered something inaudible, it sounded like she was becoming frustrated. A rubber band thwacked, in his mind he saw her replacing a batch of certificates, starting on another.

A steel drawer closed, another slid open. She was flipping faster now, he sensed her frustration.

He spotted an ashtray behind the free-standing calendar, stubbed his cigarette out in it alongside Daphne's. He resisted the temptation to light another.

Bloody well hurry up, will you? Now, that was being unfair to Daphne, she was the most efficient registrar's assistant the town had had for years.

He heard her returning footsteps, the door opening. He drew a deep breath, held it. This was the moment of truth.

Her hands were empty and his mouth went dry.

'I'm awfully sorry, Mr Edmonds.' She was clearly worried and embarrassed. 'I've been through the whole file since the beginning of the year and there's no trace of it. I *could* have mis-sorted it. If you can hang on until Monday, I'll try to find half an hour to go through the last year's file. It *has* to be here somewhere, it can't have gone anywhere.'

'Thanks, Daphne.' Edmonds tried to conceal his own frustration. 'Actually, it isn't that important,' he said, trying to make it sound casual. 'Just a technical detail, but I'll find a way round it. Don't waste any more time looking and have a good weekend.'

Because Edward Kroll's copy death certificate was not going to be found in the archives any more than the original would be found at the head office. Nor would his medical record be located in the health centre's files.

It was as if Kroll had neither lived nor died, that he did not exist.

Fourteen

Chad had been gone over two hours, it might have been three. Lindy could not remember exactly when he had left, she had been too confused to note the time.

Her anxiety was escalating into fear as she sat on the sofa; the wall clock over the mantleshelf was mocking her with its loud ticking; it seemed to be going faster than usual, as if its mechanism had gone berserk, was intent on propelling her towards some awful fate. Eleven twenty-five.

She resisted the temptation to lift the clock down, shut it somewhere where she could neither see it nor hear it; in the linen cupboard, perhaps, bury it in a heap of blankets, smother it. Or smash it into silence on the tiled hearth. It was illogical thinking, it would not help Chad any.

She should have stopped him from going. How? Once Chad's mind was made up, nobody prevented him from doing what he wanted to do. He was stubborn to the point of foolhardiness, totally inflexible. She wouldn't have had him any other way. Except now.

All right, she accepted that there was no way in which she might have dissuaded her lover from going up to Kroll's house, her conscience was clear on that score. But she should have gone with him, he *had* offered to allow her to accompany him.

She hadn't gone because she had been too bloody scared. But not as scared as she was sitting here in the flat over the bank.

Her fidgeting was becoming a writhing, stretching out her legs, pulling them back up, sitting on her feet. Her long fingernails gouged the palms of her sweaty hands.

That clock was having an hypnotic effect on her, the long

hand clicked forward, another minute of her life was gone. What was living except waiting to die? That timepiece was deliberately rushing her life away, Chad's too. He might already be dead.

Or worse.

'*Fuck you*!' she yelled at it, wrenched her body sideways, draped her legs over the end of the couch. She would find something else to look at.

The picture hung above the window that looked down on the street. For some reason the frame had tilted, slanted at a stupid angle, which gave it a totally different effect.

She had painted it herself years ago during a vacation from college. It was really good now that she looked at it objectively; with hindsight she should have taken a degree in art instead of seventeenth-century literature which had not been a grain of use to her since.

The watercolour was good, really good, she knew that now even though she had rubbished it at the time. It was Chad who had insisted on hanging it on the wall.

Chad should have been back long ago.

She recalled that day when she had painted the townscape. It had been a blistering hot August afternoon, her original intention had been to make a picture looking down Broad Street from the clocktower. She had seated herself on the plinth but the sun had been directly in her eyes so she had changed position. That had given her a different viewpoint. She had decided to paint . . . The Narrows.

It hadn't seemed creepy on that brilliant summer's day even though the steep narrow street was bathed in shadow. Kind of relaxing. Cool and inviting.

She stared, shied, lifted a hand to shield her eyes from the building which stood out more plainly from the others than she had ever noticed before. Three houses up from the Grillhouse . . .

Kroll's house.

It looked different, not so shabby as it did in real life these days; details were prominent, the front door wasn't warped and peeling, probably because she had painted it that way. The windows were dull but not grimed with dirt. Artist's licence.

Chad was inside there right now.

She got to her feet, went over to the window and parted the curtains. Lines of multi-coloured Christmas lights illuminated the snow powdered street, crossed from side to side. Like carnival weekend except that now the pavements were not lined with crowds, there was no procession, no atmosphere of gaiety. Instead, she sensed the evil that brooded over the town.

The clock on the tower struck simultaneously with the one on the wall. Midnight.

There was still no sign of Chad.

Chad had entered Kroll's house through the back door because it was the easiest means of entrance. The lock was broken, hung by a single screw, he had to use his shoulder to force the door back, it made a loud scraping noise on the uneven stone floor. He stood there trembling, listening. Kroll was sure to have heard.

If he was home. *If* he was awake. *If* he was alive.

Chad stood there inside the ramshackle porch and half considered turning around and going back outside. Whilst there was still time.

He didn't, for a number of reasons. Primarily, loss of face, Lindy might be pleased to see him back home but she'd know he had chickened out. Also, he had come this far, gained illegal entry, that was the trickiest part. Even if he left now and Kroll reported a break-in, it might be traced back to himself. Charged with breaking and entering with intent to steal. Sentenced to three months in prison, suspended for two years, if he was lucky.

He had his story prepared, had rehearsed it on the walk up to the Narrows. Two versions: if Kroll was home, then Chad would apologize, explain that he had been concerned about the other and when there had been no answer to his knocking, he'd considered it his duty to check. Of course, he *should* have called the police but he thought that Kroll would prefer not to involve the law. Maybe they'd have a cup of tea, chat, and the interview could be conducted without the old man even being aware of it. Once the tabloids had the story, tough shit!

Or if Kroll wasn't home, then Chad would have a discreet look round, write up a piece on his findings. Inside the House of Death. It wouldn't have the impact of an 'Interview with the Man From Beyond the Grave', but maybe that could come later.

And if he discovered Edward Kroll lying dead . . . He decided to concentrate on the first two options, play it as it came.

He moved through into the hallway. He had his small pocket torch in readiness but he did not need it. The reflection from the Christmas lights outside enabled him to see enough, a kind of kaleidoscopic illumination.

A thought crossed his mind, prickled the back of his neck. The curtains were open, allowing the street lighting to infiltrate the house. He had thought nothing of it at the time as he stood outside the front door waiting for his knock to be answered. He had looked up, but it had not registered then.

It was as though the drapes had been pulled back in order to light the interior enough for an intruder to see his way around.

As if Edward Kroll had been expecting him.

No, that was crazy, there was no way the man could possibly have known. He had probably pulled the curtains so that he could see the festive lights, his way of celebrating Christmas and lighting his house for free at the same time. The theory fitted and Chad breathed a sigh of relief.

God, it was cold in here, much colder than it was standing outside on the street. He checked that his anorak was zipped right up and he was wearing gloves for reasons other than just keeping his hands warm.

He looked in the kitchen. There was evidence of a snack meal having been eaten in the one space left uncluttered on the table: a tin of corned beef with the lid replaced; a pack of cracker biscuits meticulously refolded; a knife smeared with jam amidst a litter of crumbs.

Chad knew that he had to go upstairs. He moved cautiously, every board creaked beneath him, no matter how furtively he tried to move. Listening at every step, tensing. Trying to convince himself that Kroll was away somewhere, that the house was empty.

There was somebody here, all right.

He sensed it, a presence that you did not hear, did not see but you *felt* it. An invisible force that was all around, watching Chad's every move.

Waiting.

Books were piled on every stair in the way that most households placed items in readiness to be moved to an upper floor. Only these were going nowhere, they were permanent; they would remain here for ever.

He met with the stench on the landing, a foul odour that was almost tangible, had him gasping for breath which only resulted in him taking more down into his lungs. He tried not to cough. Jesus, what a stink!

He flashed his torch on and off; it was enough to show him the open lavatory door at the far end of the long corridor of books, the seat lifted. The dirty old bugger was too lazy to . . .

Chad stiffened, his ears picked up the faint sound of trickling water. The cistern was gradually refilling, an antiquated system taking its time. Which meant that . . .

Edward Kroll was somewhere around.

The reporter thought he heard a noise, could not be certain from which direction it came. Upstairs or downstairs? Was that somebody breathing? No, the night wind had found a gap beneath one of the sills, blew in icily.

The boxes of books formed a kind of maze. He followed them, emerged into a room that was shelved on all walls, just the window left to provide enough light to see by. He peered through the dusty glass, made out a series of walled yards below, recognized the Cwm in the distance. He was at the rear of the house, for a moment he had lost all sense of direction.

Chad thought that he had retraced his steps but obviously he had not because he came out into a larger room, caught his breath. It was evidently the main bedroom; an old fashioned wrought iron bedstead was heaped with unwashed sheets and blankets, a pillow propped up as though the occupant liked to read in bed. Something glinted beneath it, Chad grimaced. A huge chipped chamber pot, he guessed that it was in use.

He should never have come, he fought off a feeling of panic. Just a dirty old man's hovel, there must be thousands like this one around the country. Just filth, no story that would remotely interest a tabloid that paid its way on sensations. The rumours had originated from gossip, escalated out of all proportion. No way did anybody die and then return from the grave; it was impossible, he was too gullible, that was his problem.

Somebody definitely coughed.

Chad jumped, knocked against a pile of boxes, rocked them precariously. Somebody was out there on the main landing in one of the cardboard corridors. He almost shouted, Is that you, Mr Kroll? I was looking for you. But all the lines he had carefully rehearsed seemed ridiculous when faced with reality.

There was silence, just the stench and the cold, he tried to tell himself that he had imagined that cough. He knew he hadn't. Furthermore, he had to get out of here and forget the story!

The boxed passageways forked just outside the bedroom door. The one on the left led back to the smaller room, beyond that it got confusing. So the right-hand one probably led to the stairway, came out by that stinking toilet. Chad hoped so because he had become disoriented again.

The light from outside did not reach this far, he almost flicked on his torch. No, that would give him away for sure, he must feel his way, test every step ahead of him.

The blackness was infinite, the cold more intense than ever. An arm outstretched, the fingers clasping the torch in readiness should it be needed. Boxes all the way, the path between them was becoming narrower. And narrower.

Until Chad came to a dead end.

Fuck it, he was lost now! No, he wasn't, he pulled himself

together with an effort. Only one course was open to him, he must retrace his steps until he arrived back at that fork and then take the left-hand one. At least the smaller room was closer to the stairway and there was light there. He would be able to find his way by trial and error; if you were wrong, you turned back, tried again.

And became lost again.

Something touched him, he was unable to check his cry. Struggling to turn in the restricted space, switching on his torch.

There was nobody there. If there had been, there was nowhere for them to hide because right here the walls were straight and sheer, there were no nooks and crannies.

He had definitely felt a contact, frightening in its gentleness, the way a pevert might slyly touch a fellow passenger on a crowded train, snatch his fingers away and, if the reaction was angry, make out it had been accidental.

But that hand had been as cold as death, a corpse reaching out for a living companion.

Chad left his torch on, he wished that he had thought to fit a new battery but this one would surely suffice. Christ, he ought to be out of this house within a couple of minutes.

Except that the passage did not come out into the book lined room with the window that overlooked the Cwm. Without warning it turned sharply at right angles. And almost immediately at right angles again.

Chad hesitated, it seemed that the passage went back on itself, two parallel tunnels in a rabbit warren that might have come out just anywhere. This was crazy beyond belief!

A dim multi-coloured glow came from somewhere, seeped through cracks in the stacked carton, a hue that could only have come from the street outside. Which meant that there was a window somewhere close by; if Chad could find it then at least he would be able to get his bearings.

Even as the idea crossed his mind, the light was extinguished and everywhere was plunged back into stygian blackness.

'Shit!' He spoke his frustration aloud, noted how his torch

was dimming still further, its beam was no more than a dying glow.

Still, that light had come from somewhere on his left and there had to be a street-facing window very close. Once again he started to grope his way along the wall of boxed books, any second he *must* come upon a turn to the left.

He didn't; he had an uneasy feeling that he was following a concave, shuffling round in a circle that would bring him back to the very place whence he had started, that filthy bedroom with the chamber pot beneath the bed. He knew that any minute he would give way to blind panic, this time he would not be able to check it.

Whoosh! It was a sound like somebody was trying to blow out candles on a birthday cake. A gust of fetid arctic air fanned his cheek, had him falling up against the boxes in his terror. Something had blown at him in malevolent mischievousness for no human breath could be as cold and as foul as that vile blast.

'*Who's there? Who is it*?' His shout was close to hysteria. He stabbed the torch out at arm's length but it was spent, no brighter than the glow of a cigarette.

He heard a movement, a swishing noise like a trailing garment might make, a shuffling as though bare feet scraped along the bare boards.

Then breathing that was laboured, snuffling and gurgling, coming slowly along this maze of nightmarish, never-ending passageways, like some indescribable carnivorous hunting beast that had picked up his scent.

Charles Chadwick fled in blind panic. His useless torch fell from his fingers, rolled away somewhere. He ran, bounced off one wall of boxes on to another, scrambled back up to his feet. He was dimly aware of the taste of blood in his mouth as he blundered on with outstretched arms, pin-balled from one wall to another. Corner after corner, in his dizziness he seemed to be going uphill, then downhill.

His chest was pounding, there was a roaring in his ears but it did not shut out the wheezing breaths of whatever it was that pursued him. Sometimes it seemed to be almost upon him, other times some distance away. Like it was playing some devilish, sadistic cat-and-mouse game with him, running him until he was too exhausted to go any further.

The blackness was streaked with red, his chest would explode at any second. Pray God that he died before the creature which inhabited this foul hell caught up with him.

It smelled so strongly that he knew it was almost upon him, if he screamed then he never heard himself. Groping graveyard fingers sought a grip on his hair to pull him back but in that very instant the floor had disappeared beneath him.

It was like one of those dreams where one is falling, a staircase on which the rail eludes flailing arms; headlong, somersaulting, cartwheeling, bracing oneself for the inevitable impact. Then waking with a feeling of vertigo, surprisingly unhurt.

Chad grunted as the breath was knocked from him, crawled, only sheer desperation enabling him to move. Unseeing, sobbing, his remaining strength ebbing from him. Then lying there, eyes tightly shut so that he might not see, awaiting whatever terrible fate was to be his.

Nothing happened. It must be all part of his cruel tormentor's game. Open your eyes and look, Chad.

No!

Gradually, he became aware that something was different. The cold had not relented but the floor beneath him had a different texture; it was harder than before but slippery, so that when he attempted to move, his outstretched leg slid sideways.

Fearfully, he squinted through half-closed eyes. It was dark but not with that impenetrable blackness that had engulfed him before. In the shadowy light he could discern buildings, shop fronts and tall half-timbered buildings. The ground upon which he lay was covered with a crisp whiteness that scintillated in the light from the stars above.

With some difficulty he stood, supported himself against a stone wall. It was a dream sent to taunt him, he kept relief and euphoria at bay. Another trick played by the unseen occupant of the house that had once belonged to Edward Kroll; you flee and just when your tortured mind convinces you that you're safe . . .

He glanced fearfully behind him. Kroll's house stood dark and silent, the way it had always been. And behind every grimy window pane the curtains were closed.

The Christmas lights were dead, as was the street lighting, nothing moved on the snow-covered streets. A spook town, the domain of a bogey man, a living corpse who ruled over mortals.

And then the clock on the tower began to chime. Chad counted them. It was two o'clock on a dead morning.

Chad eased open the door of the flat, wafted the flame of a candle that burned on the mantleshelf, created weird shadows that darted away at his approach. He stood there, leaned against the lintel. He thought his ankle might be sprained, his sweatshirt was ripped.

At first he could not see Lindy, presumed that she had long gone to bed, probably soon after the power failed, left the candle for him. Then a movement down by the sofa caught his eye, a huddled shape that straightened out, a sob of whispered relief.

'Chad!'

'Lindy!' He stared as she came unsteadily towards him, she stumbled but somehow he managed to grab her.

'Oh, Chad, whatever's happened to you?'

'Not a lot.' This was no time to recount his experiences, he doubted if he ever would be able to explain them, not so that anybody would believe him, anyway.

'You're in a dreadful mess, and you've hurt yourself. You can hardly walk, your clothes are torn and you've got a split lip.'

'You don't look so good yourself.'

'Oh, Chad, it was awful.'

'Just a power failure, I guess. The lights will probably be back on by the time we get up in the morning.'

'That was just the start of it!' She was whispering, glancing about her.

'What on earth are you talking about, Lindy?'

She hesitated, then, with a shaking hand she pointed over in the direction of the window. 'Just . . . look. Oh. God, it's impossible but it's true, see for yourself!'

He looked, shook his head. 'I can't see anything wrong, the curtains are . . .'

'The picture, Chad, the one I painted when I was at college. The one you insisted on hanging over the window. For Christ's sake, can't you see?'

He stared, might have moved closer but for the fact that she was holding him back, cowering from the watercolour high upon the wall. Just looking at the Narrows started his skin prickling all over again. His mouth went dry, there was something odd about that painting, something that you'd got used to looking at daily and took for granted; something was different, he could not quite decide what it was, like those 'spot the difference' competitions they ran in the paper, two identical pictures but something had been changed in one of them. You could spend ages trying to work out what it was.

'Kroll's house!' Lindy shrieked, dug her fingernails into him as she clutched at him. 'Don't you see it, Chad? The curtains were open before, now, somehow, they're closed!'

Fifteen

The blizzard began on New Year's Eve, raged for three nights and three days before finally petering out on January third. The roads were blocked with snowdrifts level with the hedges on either side, and the relentless frosts which followed would make the thaw a slow one when eventually it came. It was the first time since 1963 that the rivers had frozen solid enough to bear the weight of an adventurous skater.

The severe frosts hampered the snow clearance crews. Blowers, which are only effective when the snowfall is fresh and powdery, stood idle. JCBs struggled to dig out the lanes, ploughs cut rutted, single tracks on the main roads. In most places access was only possible in 4x4 vehicles.

The weather forecasters offered little hope of an early let-up in the Big Freeze; it might last for weeks like it had done in 1981. A succession of mild winters created apathy; once again the Highways Department had been taken by surprise.

'Well, at least *he* won't venture outside in these conditions!' Christine Morgan spoke in a hushed whisper, almost afraid to voice her optimism in case it tempted fate.

'And neither will most other people.' John had debated whether or not to open the restaurant today but perhaps reduced hours and a depleted menu was better for morale than remaining closed. A Tuesday without Edward Kroll's regular lunchtime visit would be no small consolation.

'The boys haven't been anywhere at all this holiday and school starts again next Monday,' Christine commented as she chopped some carrots unenthusiastically. 'I was hoping to take them on a day trip to Birmingham but there's no way we'll be going now. All they've done, day after day, is play those damned computer games. And another thing, John . . .'

'Yes?' He knew only too well what she was going to say, he had been anticipating it since Christmas.

'I . . . I don't want *him* coming in here anymore. We reserve the right to refuse to serve anybody we don't want. We don't even have to give a reason. Or, if we do, it's easy enough to think one up.'

'We can't afford to turn custom away, there's precious little of it these days as it is.' It sounded a lame excuse, he couldn't think of a better one. He suddenly became very busy unwrapping a pack of smoked bacon. Because today was Tuesday. Because Tuesdays were Edward Kroll's all-day breakfast days. One could not be absolutely certain that he wouldn't come shuffling in through the door right on one forty. It was best to be prepared.

'All you have to do is to tell him, firmly but politely, that he can no longer continue to eat here.'

'And you think he'll just accept it like that?' John gave a nervous laugh. 'He'll want to know why, you know what he's like as well as I do, mutters on about every little detail.' Since Kroll's return it was always 'he' or 'him', he was never referred to by name, not just in the Grillhouse but all over the town.

'Then you'll have to tell him the truth, that nobody else will eat here when he's in here. And if you don't, then *I* will!'

'We probably won't see him for weeks, this snow looks like lying for some time,' John said as he tried to defuse the situation. 'He won't venture outside his front door. In fact, he'll probably stop in bed most days to save on the electric bill, he's told me that so many times I could scream, thinks nobody else has thought of it.'

'Well, when he does venture out, you make sure that you do tell him in no uncertain terms. Rick and Tom are terrified of him coming in here. John, you've no idea what that ghoul's done to our sons.' Her expression was anguished, there was a hint of hysteria in her shrill voice. 'They've hardly gone out of doors since . . . since he came back!'

'It's all a load of nonsense and superstition,' he sneered. 'Dr King will vouch for that, he's checked him over, so I'm told on good authority. And the bugger's alive, all right. He isn't one of the bloody walking dead.'

'Then how does the doctor explain the funeral, the burial, and him coming back to live in his house when he should by rights be in his grave? You tell me that, John, and I'll rest easy in my bed at night.'

'It's some kind of fraud, I know it is but don't ask me to explain it. Doubtless, the police will investigate it in due course, but I'll bet that funeral was a set-up and it's all something to do with evasion of inheritance tax. Some fiddle or other, but he'll get found out in the end.'

'I just hope to God that's all it is.'

'Maybe we'll never know.'

'Anyway, the next time he comes in here . . .'

'All right, all right, I'll tell him!' John Morgan's nerves were on edge, Chrissie's nagging didn't help. He understood how she and the boys were reacting because he felt that way himself. Up until now he had managed to conceal his fear from them; he would not be able to for much longer.

You sensed it with everybody, the whole town was living in terror of a man who had died and then returned from the grave. They were even blaming Edward Kroll for that power failure before Christmas; they said he hated Christmas because he was a disciple of the devil, so to spite them he had blown the coloured lights, used his terrible black magic to plunge the entire town into darkness.

It was all sheer nonsense but you believed it all the same.

John was in the process of locking the restaurant door when he heard Rick come downstairs and go through to the kitchen. A padding of shoeless feet, a deliberate furtiveness. The boy might be going to help himself to a scoop of ice cream or a glass of coke but he knew he only had to ask. It was like he had waited on the stairs until John went out of the kitchen and into the dining area. Because, for some reason, he preferred to keep out of his father's way. Definitely, there were signs of guilt in Rick's secretiveness.

'Rick?' John moved into the kitchen doorway.

'Yeah?'

'What're you up to?'

'Nothin'.'

John sighed, there were two stock answers which Rick used in these instances: nothin' or somethin'. It usually required a forceful interrogation to extract an informative reply from his son. At the moment John felt too tired, a quiet day was often more exhausting than a busy one, boredom sapped your resolve. He might have ducked enquiring further, let it pass, except that he had a vague idea of what it might all be about.

'What's 'nothin'?' Start from basics.

Rick shrugged his shoulders, his cheeks flushed slightly and he averted his eyes. 'Nothin', that's what. Me and Tom have been playing with the PlayStation all day. We ain't done nothin' wrong.'

'Steve Wyke called this afternoon whilst I was busy serving one of our only two customers. What did he want? And don't say "nothin".' His nerves were stretched, he had to be careful that he didn't take his own frustration out on the boy.

'He only wanted to borrow something.'

'Oh! What?' *And don't you dare say 'nothin'*.

'The air rifle.' Rick sucked his lips, looked away again.

'I hope you didn't lend it to him.'

Rick's foot shuffling told John that the weapon had been lent. Christ, his son hadn't even had a chance to try it out yet and now it was on loan to one of the town's worst troublemakers.

'He's bringing it back first thing in the morning, Dad.'

'And what will he have used it for in the meantime? Shooting at cats, street lamps?'

'He's going after rabbits up the Garth.'

'Poaching, in other words!'

'No, one of the farmers has asked him to shoot the rabbits, they're doing a lot of damage to young trees. Dad, Steve trained as a gamekeeper when he left school.'

'Sure, an apprenticeship that lasted four months, until they caught him selling pheasants he'd shot in the pens, with an air rifle, to some shady dealer. So they fired him and he's been unemployed ever since, making a bloody nuisance of himself round the town. They reckon it was Steve that stole that car from the garage and crashed it.'

'They *reckon*. It's all bloody supposition in this one-horse town!' Like they 'reckon' about Kroll, except that that might just be true. Rick shuddered, cast a glance towards the door, was relieved to see that it was bolted.

'I've a damned good mind to go round to the Wykes' and fetch that gun back.'

'Steve will've gone out with it. He'll be up the Garth by now.'

'In six foot plus snowdrifts?'

'They're frozen, you can walk on 'em.'

'Well, I just hope that one opens up and swallows him!' John checked his urge to slap his son, knock that smirk off his face. But that would not solve anything, it would only fuel the tension that was rising within a snowbound household. Chrissie would never forgive him. 'Well, he'd better bring it back first thing in the morning. If not, I'll be banging on his front door. And don't you ever dare lend that airgun to anybody again. Get it?'

'All right.' An infuriating half promise that meant nothing.

John Morgan watched his son slouch back upstairs. He did not relish the idea of another evening spent huddled in an overcrowded upstairs lounge watching some soap that everybody except himself appeared to be enthralled with. The stock of apple pies in the freezer needed replenishing, he would bake a batch. They were always in demand. His uneasy train of thought led to Edward Kroll. It wasn't that he was afraid of carrying out Chrissie's wishes, it was the consequences he feared.

Some time later, after darkness, John thought he heard a crashing and tinkling of breaking glass from somewhere further up the Narrows. He might have gone outside to check at any other time but tonight the front door would probably be frozen up and he would have to de-ice it in order to close it again.

It wasn't worth the bother. He satisfied his conscience by lying to himself.

Steve Wyke waited until nightfall before setting out from his council house home on Fronhir. His short gamekeeping career had taught him that rabbits came out to feed at dusk, in snowy weather when the grazing was covered over they dug down to the luscious bark of young trees. Creatures of habit, the only place you found them during the daytime was in dense undergrowth; to roll a bolting rabbit you needed a shotgun, an airgun pellet was only lethal on a sitter at close range.

Night time with a white background was ideal, you could see a feeding rabbit plainly enough. He planned his foray carefully; he found an old white sheet in the airing cupboard with which to blend his cammo jacket and faded jeans against the landscape, an old woollen balaclava with which to hide his pale features and light coloured hair. His wellington boots were holed but that didn't matter tonight, everywhere would be frozen.

At twenty he did not have any aspirations towards earning a conventional living; his father worked at a factory on the industrial estate, threatened to get him a job there but no way was Steve going to endure exhausting eight-hour shifts in a stifling, dirty workshop. His mother was employed at the supermarket, she had put his name on their ever-growing waiting list. The prospect bored him stiff, he'd find an excuse to dodge an interview if they ever called him. They weren't likely to, his work-shy reputation was too well known in the locality.

He'd get by, the way he did now. Odd-jobbing was OK, an hour or two for a few quid, mowing a snob's lawn or washing his BMW. Steve had twice been in court for petty theft, he'd be more careful not to get caught in future.

He spent a lot of time fishing, the trouble was that the trout in the river were too small, they didn't sell for much. Hunting was more profitable but you needed either a shotgun or a rifle; the police wouldn't grant him a certificate with his record so it was a waste of time applying. Unlicensed firearms didn't come easily so for the moment he would content himself with the air rifle he had borrowed from Rick Morgan. There was no hurry to return it, Rick would probably forget all about it until the thaw came and that would be weeks yet.

A rabbit sold for a pound, maybe one twenty-five if it wasn't shot up, another reason for airgunning them. A pack of 200 slugs rattled in the pocket of his jacket, he attempted to calculate their potential in monetary terms: £200 plus, less a few misses. It set the blood racing in his veins. Pity the gun was a .177, a .22 was much more deadly. Still, it was a start.

Rick, for all his schoolkid macho image, hadn't even tried the weapon out, the slugs were unopened. If Steve had been given an airgun for Christmas he'd've tested it out of the bedroom window before anybody else was up and about. There were cats aplenty on the Fronhir housing estate!

The quickest route on to the Garth was straight up the Narrows, through Market Street, up the steep lane off Offa's Road. He wrapped the airgun in the bedsheet just in case anybody saw him walking through the town, but all the streets were deserted.

Steve sniggered to himself, that was because folks were shit-scared of that silly old fucker they claimed had got up out of his grave and gone back home. What a load of balls!

Just beyond the clocktower something moved from beneath a parked snow-covered car. A prowling cat, it stopped when it heard the approach of human footfalls on the crispy snow, looked back. Already Steve was starting to unwind the torn linen from around the gun. He grinned to himself as he worked the lever, fumbled a pellet out of the pack and loaded. It was best to try the weapon out early on, for range and penetration, it would be a good guide when he found some rabbits.

The cat was suspicious, the metallic snap as the barrel was closed alerted it to danger. It was better to be safe than sorry; a series of swifts bounds took it across the road and down a side alley.

'Fuck you!' Steve hissed. He lowered the gun, looked round for something to shoot at but the starlings that usually roosted high up on the clock had sought the warmth offered beneath the eaves of the adjoining houses. Fuck them, too!

He trudged on up the steep, slippery incline, made no attempt to hide the gun. He had psyched himself up for a shot, been deprived of a target. Well, he'd fucking well find *something* to shoot at! His quick temper was aroused.

The house stood out from the rest, a kind of black void in the row, it was almost as if the driving snow had deliberately shunned it; scowling its shabbiness as if it hated the other dwellings for their neat paintwork and maintenance.

That's the place, Steve stopped, looked. He did not often come up this end of town, the stories about Edward Kroll didn't interest him. Folks got all sorts of stupid ideas, some claimed to have a resident ghost and were proud of it. Spooks were fashionable, if you didn't have one, you invented one. A kind of status symbol.

Steve's finger rested lightly on the trigger, the airgun seemed to vibrate in his hands. *Go on, fire me, I want to show you what I can do!*

The polished wooden stock was snuggling into his shoulder, the barrel swung upwards, arced; the sight looked for an alignment. Perhaps there were starlings roosting in the eaves; if there were, they kept well hidden in the shadows, didn't move or twitter. A length of guttering hung down; the gun moved on. Searching, eager.

Pull! A command yelled from somewhere inside Steve's head, he sensed his finger taking a pressure on the trigger, squeezing. It was of no consequence where the barrel pointed; he felt the released compression, the thud of the spring, a faint recoil.

Glass cracked, shattered. Steve leaped back, lost his footing on the slippery surface and fell. Jagged shards hurtled downwards, splintered on the ice, powdered. Fragments glinted in the frosty starlight.

Miraculously, Steve Wyke was unscathed.

Fucking hell. He picked himself up, stared at the window above. There was a gaping hole in the pane, an inverted half moon shape that was reminiscent of a mouth that screamed in pain and anger.

Steve looked about him, no doors opened, no windows went up. Nobody came to investigate. If the residents had heard the breaking glass, they were ignoring it.

He could not remain here. A moment of stupid impulse could have dire consequences. He was breathing heavily, his feet slipped on the icy road. Hurrying, not daring to look behind him, only slowing when he reached the bottom of the drifted lane that led up on to the Garth.

There had been no pursuit, that was incredible. Nobody had seen him, nobody would be able to prove who had shot out Kroll's window. Steve laughed into the freezing night air.

The airgun had proved itself; it had sufficient power and accuracy to kill an unsuspecting rabbit.

The uphill trek was more difficult than Steve had envisaged. If the snow had not frozen solid he would have been forced to abandon his quest. No attempt had been made by the snow ploughs to clear a track up to the Garth, main roads were a priority, little used lanes would be left until last.

In some places it was impossible to determine where the roadside hedges ended and the fields began; the drifts were firm, frozen snow crunched beneath him.

The reflected whiteness and the wan starlight gave him all the light he needed, familiar trees acted as landmarks. A dark fir wood was silhouetted against the horizon, that was his intended destination, that was where the rabbits had their warrens.

He paused for breath, looked back whence he had come. Way below him Knighton nestled in the valley between the mountains, a shadowy array of buildings where nothing moved. Sinister, forbidding, it was as though he had escaped from it, had to keep going until it was hidden from his view.

He shivered, the sweat on his body was beginning to chill

him, he had to keep on the move. The weight of the gun in his hands was comforting, gave him a feeling of invincibility.

He unfolded the sheet, located the hole which he had torn in the centre, pulled it over his head. Now he was invisible, a night hunter in search of prey. His bloodlust had a warming effect on his body, the urge to kill gave him new strength.

The forest was dark and silent as if every creature that had once inhabited it had fled before the blizzard. Or lay dead and buried beneath the deep snow. Steve's optimism waned, there were always rabbits in plenty here, where had they gone?

He moved forward, his feet made a noise as if he walked on crispy, sugared breakfast cereal, crackling loudly in the stillness. Shit, if anything lived here it would hear his approach long before he could creep within range of it.

He stood in a patch of shadow, tried to work out a plan of action. Maybe the snow was not so deep beneath the trees and he would be able to move more stealthily. But it was too dark to see in the forest.

Then he saw the rabbit, stiffened. It came up over a drift some thirty metres away, appeared huge in the ethereal light, maybe twice the size it should have been. A trick of the light, surely, but it was a big one, all right. He trembled slightly with anticipation.

It was coming towards him, it had not heard him, had no idea that he was there. It had probably ventured out on to the snowy fields in search of a clump of uncovered grass, was now returning to its burrow. It moved awkwardly, slowly. But it was heading this way!

Steve had the airgun up to his shoulder, his finger rested on the trigger. He resisted the temptation to shoot; let it get closer. Closer still.

He followed its progress with the barrel sight. The rabbit stopped, sat up on its haunches, seemed to be sniffing the air. Maybe it had heard him, or scented him. Any second it might bolt away and his chance would be gone. Surely it was within range now.

Shoot!

Steve let out a shout of triumph as the creature fell back, rolled and kicked frantically, pedalling the air with all four legs. Twisting, writhing; squealing pitifully.

'Got you, you bastard!'

Steve ran forward, trod on the trailing sheet and fell forward. He cursed, scrambled back on to his feet. Somehow the wounded rabbit was standing up; it bounded away, rolled over again.

'Come back, fuck you!'

Steve tried to run, the folds of the sheet impeded him again and he tore at it, ripped a piece away. The rabbit hopped, again just out of his reach.

'I'll fix you!' He levered the gun open, fumbled with the slugs; the pack upended, spilling out on to the frozen ground; the slugs bounced, scattered like processed peas. 'Shit!' He managed to pick one up with numbed fingers, loaded the weapon. His arms were shaking, it was difficult to draw a bead.

A *phut* that did not sound right. The creature did not even flinch.

Steve examined the airgun, the problem was only too obvious. In his haste to catch his prey he must have jammed the barrel into a drift and compacted it with snow. The pellet had stuck, he might need a length of wire to prise it free.

The rabbit seemed to have revived, it was hopping, crawling, even in an injured state it was able to keep ahead of him, travelling back the way it had come.

'I'll get you if it's the last thing I do!' His vow fogged the air. Sooner or later the rabbit must tire, it clearly was not intent on making it to the wood where it might have eluded him in the darkness beneath the trees. Of course, a sudden thought, the old quarry wasn't far from here and there was a colony of rabbits living in the long discontinued slate workings. This one had come from there, obviously, and was now trying to return home to die.

Steve was sweating, he removed the rest of the constricting bedsheet, threw it to one side, pulled his balaclava off. The snowy landscape was clearly visible, he could not quite remember how far the quarry was. It had to be quite close, he could not chance the rabbit beating him to it and disappearing into some hole beyond his reach.

The animal was tiring, that much was clear; a couple of hops and then it flopped down, its flanks expanding and contracting like a pair of bellows. A trail of dark droplets signified that it was bleeding. It could not last much longer. Steve tensed himself for a headlong rush, prepared to dive on it, pin it down. Christ, I'm really going to enjoy screwing your bloody neck for you after all this!

The rabbit was maybe two metres from him, watching him with frightened, pleading eyes. It would not go any further, it was finished.

But Steve was not going to rush the coup de grâce. This little bleeder had really fucked him up; the airgun was jammed and useless, he'd lost all his slugs and his only reward for his night's work was going to be one rabbit. *This* rabbit!

'You're really gonna suffer, shitbag!' He moved slowly, took a step forward, laughed aloud at the way the creature cowered and trembled.

His laugh came back at him on the night wind but it did not sound quite right, kind of old and rasping. Somehow it must have echoed in the stillness, become distorted.

He laughed again crazily, took another step. The snowdrift on which he stood tilted, he thought it dropped a little. Frozen snow sometimes did that if there was a vacuum under it, found its own level.

He teetered, gasped. His feet sank, he went in up to his knees. A crunching, cracking sound, it was like standing on plate glass that was beginning to break up. A moment of panic, he tried to extricate himself.

That was when the ground beneath him gave way, plunged downwards, took him with it. Rushing down an icy shaft, trying to grab a hold but he was falling too fast and the sides were sheer and slippery with ice.

Steve Wyke screamed loud and long, a shriek that shattered the silence of a freezing winter's night, echoed on and on across the mountains, finally dying away in a whisper of manic, gloating laughter.

The ground trembled in the aftermath of an avalanche of frozen snow and then became still again. The rabbit writhed in one last spasm of agony, rolled over the brink of the deep, dark drop and hurtled down in the wake of its tormentor.

Sixteen

PC Phil Morris was convinced by nine a.m. that this was definitely going to be one of *those* days. These occasions always seemed to save themselves up for Sergeant Davison's off-duty periods.

Miss Wilkins from the Narrows phoned to complain that a section of pavement outside 'the house opposite' had not been cleared of snow since the blizzard, and the frost had made it an 'additional hazard'.

Phil was tempted to advise her to walk on the opposite side of the street but thought better of it. When Betty Wilkins was in one of her complaining moods she was quite likely to phone the chief inspector at Llandrindod Wells to report an officer for rudeness. It wasn't worth the hassle.

'Who is the occupant of the house, Miss Wilkins?' He held the handset a couple of inches away from his ear.

'*Him*!' Instead of the anticipated irate shriek it was a barely audible whisper.

It wasn't worth pushing it, not where Betty was concerned. He thought of a convenient let-out, a place to pass the buck. 'As a matter of fact, Miss Wilkins, uncleared pavements do not come under police jurisdiction, they are a council matter. I suggest that you telephone the Highways Department and report the matter to them, they'll send somebody out to see to it.'

'Can't *you* see to it, officer?'

'I'm afraid not. Unless, of course, the council specifically request that I go and speak to the occupant of the house, and they will only do that if he refuses to clear his area of pavement.'

'*He* won't co-operate, I can promise you that.'

'In which case they'll send somebody out to clear the obstruction and caution him for the future.'

'All at the rate payer's expense. I object to paying to have *his* snow shovelled when he's legally obliged to see to it himself.'

Jesus Christ!

'Oh, and another thing, constable.'

'Yes, Miss Wilkins.' He didn't care if she did hear his sigh.

'One of his windows is broken, there would still be glass all over the street now except that Mr Morgan kindly cleared it up. He didn't have to, he's that kind of man.'

'Then there's no problem.'

'I heard it smash yesterday evening. Vandals.'

'You saw them?'

'No, but I heard them. It was probably the Morgan boys and that's why their father cleared up the mess. Done with a catapult, if you ask me.'

I'm not bloody asking you. 'If the householder makes a complaint, then I shall investigate it.'

'I think you're deliberately dodging the issue, officer. It could just as easily have been *my* window. Why don't you go and see *him*?'

'I don't have any reason to and, anyway, you haven't yet told me who it is that hasn't cleared his snow away and whose window it is that's been broken.'

There was a long silence. These days nobody mentioned Edward Kroll by name. 'Well, officer, after I've spoken to the council I'm going to phone the chief inspector at Llandrindod Wells and demand that *somebody* goes and questions *him*. After all, he's supposed to be dead!'

Phil hardly had time to breathe another long sigh after replacing the handset before the phone rang again. This time he knew that he'd have to go out, the Wykes were reporting their son as missing. Bloody hell, that guy was a constant pain in the butt. In all probability he had stayed overnight somewhere. He was an adult, he could look after himself. All the same, you dared not chance it, just in case . . .

* * *

Steve Wyke was definitely missing. His mother, who didn't give a damn about her son's whereabouts on those occasions when she should have done, was on the verge of hysteria. Her husband, who spent more time in the bars than in his own home, was looking for an excuse to blame the police; Steve had run away from home due to police harassment, it was *their* job to find him.

Phil hoped fervently that Steve Wyke had run away and would not be returning. In the meantime, he had to make some kind of a search; he called the chief inspector. Damn it, that layabout was going to get the full rescue treatment, they were sending the police helicopter because the drifts were too deep to search the countryside on foot.

It really was turning out to be one of those days.

'Well, Steve Wyke hasn't brought your air rifle back!' John Morgan stamped angrily into the attic bedroom which Rick and Tom shared. It was eleven thirty a.m. and they showed no signs of getting up. 'And, according to what I've heard, he's gone missing overnight and they're sending a police helicopter to search for him. I guess your airgun's wherever he is and you can kiss it goodbye.'

'*You* said –' Rick's eyes peered over his bedsheet – 'that you hoped that a snowdrift opened up and swallowed him!'

'I don't expect it'll be quite as bad as that.' John felt slightly uneasy. 'He might've got lost in the mountains and they'll find him shivering but unharmed. They'll probably give him a few days living in luxury in hospital. And your gun will never be found, *that* will probably be lost in a snowdrift. Anyway, I think it's time you both got dressed and came downstairs.'

'All right.' Rick also sensed that it was going to be one of those days.

'Oh, and by the way, somebody broke one of Mr Kroll's windows yesterday evening. An upstairs one, I heard the glass shatter. It might have been done with an airgun!'

John slammed the bedroom door behind him and went back downstairs.

* * *

The two police officers peered down into the dark depths of the hole in the snowdrift. They lay flat, the frozen surface was not to be trusted. A hundred metres behind them their helicopter stood on an icy plateau like some gigantic vulture that had scented carrion and landed to investigate.

'It might be a sheep.' The younger of the two was looking for an excuse not to have to go down there.

'Could be,' the sergeant agreed, 'on the other hand it could be a human. The heat sensor says there's sommat down there so we have to find out what it is. Otherwise there's no point in making a search, is there?'

'I suppose not.'

'We'd better radio Mountain Rescue, it looks a deep one.' Their lamp beams didn't reach the bottom but that was probably because there was a bend in the snow shaft.

'We're on an old quarry, aren't we, sarge?'

'Could be but it's difficult to pinpoint landmarks when the whole countryside's under deep snow.'

The younger man felt weak with sudden relief. At least he wasn't going to have to go down *there*. These mountain guys were used to it, it wouldn't be any problem to them.

The rescue unit answered the call within minutes, there was an eagerness about the red and white chopper itself even. Banner was a big man in every respect, the policemen found themselves wondering how much of him there was when he took his protective clothing off; a giant of a man, all you saw was a black beard, deep blue eyes. His companion was smaller, worked the ropes and the winch, kept in touch by radio.

Banner stared down into the depths, adjusted the lamp on his helmet. 'An old quarry shaft, been there for a century, maybe. You only notice it because everywhere else is stark white, you wouldn't see it at all if the snow had drifted over it.'

The young police officer shuddered at the other's words. A hill walker would step right on to a slender covering . . . It was probably a fox or a sheep, like the sarge said. He almost convinced himself, not quite.

Somehow Banner slid into the hole with ease, his companion unravelling the rope; it tautened, slackened, tautened again.

It was just beyond the first bend that his feet touched an obstruction, like a bar wedged across the shaft, maybe an old support; it felt like it was coming loose, he could shift it easily enough. He shone his hand torch downwards, the beam glinted on polished metal, there was no sign of rust. It had bowed, twisted, was held horizontally by a triangular piece of polished woodwork.

It was an air rifle.

Banner pushed with a booted foot, the weapon broke free, went clattering on down. He paused, rested his back against the slate wall, began to count. He reached five before he heard the gun thud to a halt.

Another thirty feet and he would be on the bottom.

There was a final convex that hid the floor from his view, the tunnel was widening here. In all probability it levelled out, formed a passageway, maybe a maze of them. During the last century minerals had been mined here, the top slate was an added bonus. Primitive extraction methods led to accidents, roof falls; the old miners had left a legacy for the present generation.

Banner descended into what appeared to be a circular pit, the bottom had filled with water but it had frozen, formed a slippery surface that bore his weight. Well, if anything had fallen down the shaft, it had to be right here.

It was.

He started as he turned around, recoiled with a muttered cry that echoed eerily in the confined space. If there had been room he would probably have backed off. But there wasn't.

The guy was dead, all right, anywhere else he would have been a huddled, bloody corpse. He had died as he had slipped, rigid as a jack, rigor mortis that had not thawed out. A frozen stiff, he laughed at his own joke, a mountain rescuer had to have his own sense of humour to remain sane. Even so, it was borderline sanity.

Dead frightened eyes met his own out of a blood encrusted face, the lips had glued together. A head injury, in all probability, that wasn't Banner's problem. He started to fix the spare rope, it would uncoil with him as Tad hauled him back up. Ten minutes flat and they'd have this jerk in a body bag and on its way to the mortuary.

He knotted the rope, pulled it tight. There was an awful lot of blood, too much, possibly a main artery had been severed.

As he straightened up, he only just managed to check his scream, and Banner hadn't screamed since he was a kid. The open throat leered at him, grinned, a wound that ran the length of the neck with bloody lips and protruding from it was what appeared to be a huge shard of glass.

Jesus, it was like somebody had slit his fucking throat!

Banner signalled to be hauled up. The sooner he was out of this place, the better.

He heard the corpse bumping and thudding its way up behind him, almost as if it was in pursuit. Something cracked loudly, tinkled all the way down to the bottom.

The weapon of death had snapped.

Seventeen

'Bloody great!' The driver of the snowplough slammed his radio handset back into its cradle. 'I bloody ask you!'

'What's up?' His grey-haired companion took a loud slurp of tea, clutching the thermos mug in search of warmth. 'Don't tell me we gotta go back up to Llandod!'

'Na', wish we bloody 'ad,' the florrid-faced operator complained as he rustled another sandwich out of the bread wrapper on the cab facia ledge. 'At least then we might be doin' sommat useful. I was hoping to finish this stretch down into Presteigne today, another three or four hours would see it off. A main bloody road, traffic needs it. So, guess what?'

'What?' The other was unmoved. He obeyed orders, no matter what, that way you finished your week and picked up your pay packet and nobody could criticize you. The trouble with Dai was that he thought he should have been a foreman but he was all mouth and the bosses knew it.

'We gotta break off, go into Knighton in the Land Rover and shovel snow and ice from off the pavement in front of somebody's 'ouse. And the boss says to be quick about it in case somebody slips and breaks a leg, sues the council. I bloody ask you!'

'Why don't the householder do it 'imself?' It seemed a reasonable enough question to ask.

'Ah!' Dai's thick forefinger went up, his expression was one of disbelief. 'The Highways and Transport Department,' he said affecting a cultured tone, 'don't even know whose house it is. A woman rang in to complain yesterday. *Yesterday*! The message has slowly filtered up to the top and now they're shitting themselves in case it might be too late. "Go as quick as you can, Mr Davies and take Tricklebank with you." Rules are that it has to be two to a job.'

'I could've carried on ploughing the road, Dai.'

'Not on yer own, you can't. Two to a job, you should know that, Fred.'

''Ow can we shovel the snow off'n some bugger's house if we don't know which bloody house it is?' That seemed an even more reasonable question. Fred braced himself for the answer to it.

'We 'ave to go see the woman what complained.' Dai took a last swig of tea, screwed the top back on his flask. 'She'll tell us which one. Provided she's 'ome, of course. If she's out shopping then we come back here and carry on snow clearing. That's the way we work around here and I didn't think up the rules. Better lock the machine up.'

'There was sommat on the radio about an accident up in the hills above Knighton. I just catched the end bit whilst you was checking the blade, Dai.'

'Oh?' Dai Davies bumped the yellow council Land Rover over a frozen rut. 'What's that, then?'

'Some feller got lost, fell down a disused mine shaft. And just in case the fall didn't kill 'im, one of them stalactine things cut 'is bloody throat for 'im.'

'*Stalactites*!' The driver never missed an opportunity to demonstrate any knowledge which he had. 'A length of ice, caused by condensation or water dripping and freezing. Poor bugger!'

'Beats me what anybody could be doing up in the hills in this weather.' Fred Tricklebank fastened the toggles on his duffle coat, the old Land Rover was draughty, not snug and warm like the snowplough.

It seemed an awfully long journey just to go and shovel up a barrowful of snow. He wondered why they had to send two county council workmen when every town had a force of district council roadmen. He gave up, it wasn't any of his business.

Betty Wilkins was a big woman. At least, the figure the two workmen could see through the narrow gap in the open door was of a large woman. She might even have been bigger still. She was wearing a housecoat as if she had only just got up out of bed and the sash was straining to meet.

'Can I help you, gentlemen?' Her voice was as disagreeable as her expression, she clearly regarded this call as an intrusion upon her mid-morning privacy.

'We've come about the snow on the pavement.' Dai could not see any snow except for the compacted, slippery surface of the street.

'Oh . . .' Puzzlement merged into understanding, she had probably forgotten all about yesterday's complaint. 'Oh, yes, that's it over there.'

The workmen's heads turned, they stared. Just outside the dilapidated doorway immediately opposite there was a slight rise of hard-packed snow where passers-by had compressed it with their feet. You did not notice it until you looked closely.

'Is that *all*?' Dai grunted, calculating valuable snow-ploughing time that had been lost. 'God blimey, it'll be worn away by this afternoon!'

'It's dangerous. Remove it, please.'

'Who lives in that 'ouse?' Dai worked by the rule book. It was the occupant's responsibility to clear any obstruction immediately adjacent to his premises whether leaves or snow. He must be informed that the job was being carried out on his behalf by the county authority and that he would probably be charged for the work.

'I've no idea.'

'No idea!' He made no attempt to hide his incredulity. 'Stone me, you live four metres from 'is front door and you don't know who he is!'

Mrs Wilkins seemed to shrink back into the interior of her hallway, the door began to close. 'I have no idea and, furthermore, I'm not interested. Please clear that snow before somebody is injured!'

The door slammed shut and the two bewildered men looked at each other.

'Charmin'. Fred, go and knock on that door, tell the bloke

what we've come to do and that 'e should've done it 'isself. I'll go fetch the barrow and shovels.'

Dai Davies walked slowly up the pedestrianized street to where the Land Rover was parked beyond the concrete bollards. It was time Fred learned to speak up for himself, you couldn't go through life just obeying orders. And Dai would take the opportunity to have another drink from his flask whilst Fred sorted out the preliminaries. He laughed to himself at the thought.

'Well?' Davies parked the barrow, saw that his companion stood uneasily in front of the house, was clearly agitated.

'I don't think there's anybody home.'

'How many times've you knocked?'

'Three but I can't make anybody hear.'

'You want to bloody thump, not tap.' Dai Davies affected a swagger, pushed past his companion. 'Now, this is 'ow it's done . . .'

Even as the burly workman drew back his huge clenched fist, the door began to scrape open; an inch or two at a time as though it was having to be forced. A figure stood in the open space, so slight that the shabby coat seemed to hang from his sloping shoulders. But there was no way that the brim of the greasy hat could hide those wasted, ill-tempered features.

'Jesus Almighty!' Dai Davies was unable to check his surprise.

'What is going on?' The voice seemed to crackle like static electricity in the frosty air, a near-fleshless finger pointed accusingly.

'We've come about the . . .' Davies's bluster had become a stammer. 'About the . . . this lump o' frozen snow. Somebody might slip on it, break a leg.'

'*I* never asked you to call.'

'No, er . . . well, you see, it's like this . . .'

'*Who* summonded you?'

They stepped back, Tricklebank might have fled except that he would have been ridiculed by his companion, the story told amidst guffaws in the workmen's mess back at Llandrindod Wells. Dai didn't seem too confident now, though.

'There . . . there was a complaint phoned in . . .'

'By *whom*?'

Dai swallowed, his coarse ruddy complexion had gone several shades paler. 'That . . . that woman over there.' He half-turned, pointed with a trembling finger.

Tricklebank looked, willed the door opposite to open and Mrs Wilkins to emerge, take responsibility. But the studded door with its tiny bottled glass window remained closed.

'Mrs Wilkins complained, did she?' Edward Kroll was muttering to himself but his expression was terrible to behold. The skin over his cheekbones was stretched so that it might have ripped, the mouth was a thin, angry line. His eyes seemed to burn in their deep, dark sockets.

'We're just doin' what we was told to do,' Dai gulped uncharacteristically. 'The boss said . . .'

'Well, go back and tell your boss that *I* don't want you shovelling outside my house.'

'I'm sorry, guv.' Davies shuffled, looked down at his heavy, scuffed working boots. 'But we 'ave to do it. You could get prosecuted for not clearing your frontage. I know a chap once who refused and . . .'

'*Go . . . away*!'

'Maybe we should radio back to headquarters, Dai, ask 'em to send the chief out.'

'Na'.' the other took a deep breath pulled himself together. 'We gotta do it, Fred. 'Ere –' he reached behind him, lifted a shovel out of the wheelbarrow – 'get shovellin'.'

'*Stop*!'

The cry, a shrill shriek of demonaic fury, almost stopped them. Almost. Except that Fred Tricklebank had his orders and he never disobeyed. He bent forward, chopped and scraped with the heavy tool, sliced off a chunk of compressed frozen snow. The rest had loosened, came away in a single, jagged triangular piece, broken up as it thudded in the barrow. The sound of scraping, steel on concrete filled the air, a noise that jarred already shaken nerves. Neither man even glancing up until the job was finished.

'There, Mr . . .'

Kroll had shrunk back into the shadows of his hallway,

a spectre in the dark that was clearly displeased. He seemed to shimmer, he was probably shaking with fury.

'Somebody's broke yer window.' Davies noticed that a shard of glass glinted in the barrow amidst the crumbled ice. He looked up, saw the smashed pane. 'You want to get that fixed afore the rest falls out, could go and cut somebody badly.'

'I hear that the culprit has already paid for his foolishness,' Kroll whispered and was scarcely audible yet it had the two workmen backing away towards their barrow. 'You, also, have been extremely foolish, acting upon a trivial complaint from that dreadful woman. But . . .' A sigh that rattled Kroll's lungs. 'What is done, is done. It cannot be undone.'

They did not look back, had the feeling that those sunken eyes watched them all the way up to the top of the Narrows.

Dai's hand shook as he started the Land Rover. 'A lot of bloody unpleasantness over nothing,' he muttered as he pulled out into the snow-packed road. 'Still, I don't expect we'll ever see that bloke again and that'll be too soon. Like a bloody ghoul, he was!'

'I'd better check that blade before we start again, Fred.' They were back at the snowplough, the giant machine stood silent with its blade upraised. 'It seems a bit loose, don't give you a clean sweep on the offside. I'll just check the nuts.' He started the engine, let it tick over.

Fred climbed up into the cab, reached for his flask. Dai wouldn't let him operate, never did. It was always: 'get ready with them cones, Fred, put 'em out when we're round that bend, just in case some silly bleeder comes pilin' into the back of us' or 'watch that side so's I don't cut the verge up too much'. Every workman was required to have a mate, according to the rule book, even if that mate did nothing all day.

Dai was always tinkering with the equipment, whatever it was, even when it had come straight from the maintenance yard. Fred sipped his tea, listened to the clinking and tapping as his companion loosened or tightened nuts, or just did something for the hell of it.

'Now lower the blade, Fred, let me check it for alignment.'

Bloody hell, not a moment's peace to drink your flamin' tea. 'All right, hang on.'

Fred reached across, grasped the lever. It was tight, he needed to exert force, slopped his tea. The big blade would lower slowly, clank all the way.

It came down fast in one sudden fall with a thud that vibrated the cab, slopped more tea. It had never dropped like that before. Still, it was solid enough, it shouldn'tve done any damage.

'That OK?' It wouldn't be OK, Dai would be shouting and swearing, blaming his colleague.

Dai didn't cuss, that old bloke seemed to have unnerved him and it took a lot to unsettle the snowplough operator. Fred peered out of the windscreen, all he could see was the big blade, Dai was probably kneeling down, checking that it lay level on the ground.

Fred drank the rest of his tea. He wasn't going to interfere, let the silly blighter play at maintenance if he wanted to. Don't give him the satisfaction of asking him what he was doing so that you had to listen to a detailed explanation of bullshit.

All the same, Dai was taking his time. He hadn't gone and had a bloody heart attack, had he? Or a stroke? Fred opened the door, climbed down.

'You all right, Dai?'

There was no answer. Fred walked round the front of the machine, stared aghast at the bright crimson that was spreading across the dazzling white compacted snow, soaking into it. Seeing the outstretched legs, the prone body with its heavy working coat over orange overalls. Then blood, and more blood, a sluggish flow of it oozed from beneath the lowered snowplough blade.

Fred Tricklebank's vision blurred, streaked with red. His veined hands clutched at the heavy blade for support because he knew he was going to faint.

He screamed aloud, a hoarse yell that rasped the silence of the sunlit, freezing afternoon air. '*Oh, my Christ, it's cut 'is bloody 'ead orf*!'

Eighteen

Betty Wilkins had never married because she had spent her entire life looking after her parents, and she made sure that everybody was aware of that.

It was true. An only child, her father was fifty-six when she was born, her mother thirty-three. As they aged they relied more and more upon her. 'You don't *need* to marry, Betty,' her mother had once told her. 'You've got a good teaching job and they'll surely appoint you headmistress after old Courtney retires, and you'll have an even better salary with a teacher's pension at the end of it. Plus your state pension, of course. And,' she said affecting a confidential whisper, 'your father and I will leave you comfortable. You don't want to be cooking and washing for some man, being at his beck and call when he's old and ill. You enjoy your life. Besides, *we* couldn't manage without you around. I can't drive and your father isn't as safe as he might be on the roads.'

Betty's father died of emphysema when he was seventy-eight; Dr King had bluntly remarked that he'd no business living to that age on twenty fags a day. Betty's mother had gone to pieces after her husband's death but had lingered on in ill health right up to three years ago.

Only then did Betty realize how she had wasted her life. She became embittered when it was her own turn for retirement. She was more than comfortably off but what was it worth? Money was no remedy for loneliness.

She registered with a marriage bureau; it was a sheer waste of two hundred pounds. She met several men; they were either years older than herself, seeking companionship in the twilight of their lives, or looking for somebody to cook and clean for them. Just like Mother had warned her. One man *might* just have suited but it was soon clear what *he* was after! Betty wasn't having any of *that*, it was something that had aroused her curiosity in her younger days but as the years went by her interest in sex had waned. She'd never tried it with a man and she damned well wasn't going to now!

She was sixty-eight now. She tried to look at herself objectively in the full length wardrobe mirror. She had always had a weight problem, maybe with determination she could have shed a few pounds but she had always diverted her energy into other things, like teaching and giving music lessons after school. Even now she still had a couple of pupils but it seemed that the younger generation were no longer interested in anything that improved their minds. Children didn't read for pleasure any longer, television was to blame for that; videos were even worse. Those Morgan boys were classic examples of how modern society had discarded anything of value.

It was sad, particularly so because they were intelligent boys, came from a good home. They were capable of achieving good grades in their GCSEs, there was still time, but they rejected learning. Educational suicide.

Mickey Farrell's death had devastated the schoolkids, some of them would never get over it. Betty glanced apprehensively out of the window, shuddering at the sight of the house immediately opposite.

That dreadful man had cast a cloak of fear over the entire community. Of course, logically, he could not be blamed for Mickey's death, he had been nowhere around at the time. All the same, his return after his supposed death was puzzling but it was obviously all due to some big mistake. If Kroll was dead, then the man living in his house was a twin brother. Surely that fact could be verified.

Now there were more whispered rumours. The Wyke boy had been found dead up in the hills, he'd fallen down an old quarry shaft, a stalactite had cut his throat. Betty had been shopping in the Costcutter store, strained her ears to catch what a huddle of housewives were saying.

'*He* killed Steve Wyke, you know. Because Stevie shot his window out with an airgun. You upset *him* and he'll get you, some way or other. And, if you ask me, he did that council worker, too.'

'That's rubbish, Millie, that's stretching it beyond belief. Why on earth would he want to kill somebody who doesn't even live in the town? The fellow came from Llandod.'

'There was a bit of a row, so I'm told. This bloke and his mate were sent to shovel some snow from outside *his* house. He objected. Anyway, the accident happened soon after, the snowplough blade fell on the fellow.' She spoke in a frightened whisper now. 'Cut his head right off, just like he'd been guillotined!'

One of the women blanched, looked furtively around. Sometimes Edward Kroll came in here to purchase his meagre rations. 'It's all so trivial, the chap was only doing his job.'

'It's like anybody who offends him is . . .' She left the sentence unfinished. 'They were saying in Ginger's –' another glance around but Betty was out of sight behind a rack of breakfast cereals – 'that it was Betty Wilkins who reported the uncleared snow.'

'Oh, dear!'

Betty's stomach griped, she felt a little sick.

'That's right, I can believe it, too. It was her who shopped that fellow for not licensing his lorry.'

'Well, that serves him right, we wouldn't be paying as much for our licenses if it wasn't for the dodgers. Cheats, they are, I've no sympathy.'

'That's right, but it makes you think. If *he* gets to know that it was Betty who reported him . . .'

Betty experienced a moment of dizziness. Mrs Hughes had obviously been opening her big mouth in Ginger's. Betty wished that she hadn't told her. Well, she hadn't, she'd only said that she'd a good mind to ring the council about that patch of frozen snow. Anyway, Kroll couldn't possibly know about it, could he? Unless he'd seen the council workers at her door asking where the obstruction was. Even then, it was no proof that she'd reported him. It was feasible that workmen sent to do a job in a strange locality asked directions from local residents.

Betty tried to convince herself that there was nothing to worry about. But she couldn't get the nagging fear out of her mind.

Betty had a secret that she would not have confided to another soul. Indeed, she was ashamed of it. Since her retirement she had become hooked on television soaps; *Neighbours* and *Home and Away* gave her an escape to a land of sun and warmth, far removed from the snow and fogs of Knighton; *EastEnders* and *Coronation Street* provided an affinity with an ordinary community, which she had not ever personally experienced. School functions, parents' evenings and nativity plays were always so formal. It wasn't that she felt she was superior to the townsfolk, rather that she had nothing to offer other than polite conversation. They didn't discuss literature or music, she had no idea how to make small talk. She had nothing in common with her neighbours; it had nothing whatsoever to do with class distinction.

She had become a loner, her only affinity with everyday people was through the soaps. Often she watched the repeats, too. But she always closed the curtains during these viewing times. If a passer-by chanced to glance through the window and saw her watching her favourite programme, it would be the talk of Ginger's and the Clocktower Teashop where she called for a cup of tea two or three times a week. Those were social occasions in an abstract way; she needed company but at a distance, listening to gossip but not participating in it. In a way it was a real life version of the soaps. You walked away from it afterwards.

Tonight there was another repeat of *Prisoner Cell Block H* being shown; the television company had been forced to repeat the series, there had been a national outcry when its demise was announced. Betty had been one of the thousands who had written in and complained. Whatever would Mother and Father have thought of her! An awful thought struck her: suppose they knew, wherever they were. They'd be ashamed to think that a daughter of theirs could sink to such depths. Or perhaps they would understand that she was lonely, needed company.

Cell Block night was her one late night of the week, she stayed in bed an extra hour the following morning to make up for her indulgence. She had never been used to late nights, seldom went out after tea unless it was to a school function and they seldom went on later than nine thirty.

Betty switched on the television in readiness, went through to the kitchen to make a bedtime drink. Always cocoa; she'd drunk it nightly since she was a child, remembered the old slogan: 'Cadbury's Cocoa Makes Strong Men Stronger'. It was even more comforting since Mother had gone, a link with her childhood. Usually, she took her mug of cocoa up to bed, on Cell Block nights she drank it in front of the television.

A programme was just finishing, then there would be the adverts; there was no immediate hurry. The milk boiled, she poured it on to the powder, stirred it to a brown froth.

Somebody was talking, a child's voice. She tried to remember which advertisement it was.

'I'm here.'

It sounded almost real, as good as stereo TV. Her skin prickled, it was probably cold here in the kitchen, the heating system was programmed to cut out at ten o'clock. The weather forecasters said it was going to be minus ten degrees tonight. She shivered.

'I'm here.'

That *definitely* wasn't the television. Betty turned slowly. There was an awful smell coming from somewhere, like something was rotting. Maybe a mouse had died behind the kitchen units or under the floorboards. But that did not account for that shrill childlike voice.

'*I'm here*!' It was a petulant shriek, this time as if the caller was becoming impatient because she had not gone to answer the shout. It seemed to be coming from upstairs and that stench was definitely drifting downstairs. But nobody could get in the house, all the doors and windows were fastened.

Betty knew that she had to go and look.

Even as she walked through to the hallway she sensed that somebody was standing on the landing. She thought she heard an intake of breath followed by a stealthy movement.

'Who . . . who is it?'

There was no answer. Even the television in the front room was silent as if it had somehow switched itself off. That smell seemed even stronger, had her wrinkling her nose in disgust.

'If there's anybody there, you'd better show yourself.' *No, please, I don't want to see you, not if you stink like that.*

Betty managed to control her rising panic. Directly ahead of her, on the small table against the wall, stood the telephone. If she made a dash for it she could perhaps summon help before whoever was up there could stop here.

Suppose there was nobody upstairs, that it was all in her imagination. PC Morris was getting very fed up with her lately. Anyway, the Knighton station would be closed now, all calls were transferred directly to Llandrindod Wells. It might take some time before help could reach her. First, she had to find out if there really was somebody upstairs.

Nervously, she approached the foot of the stairs. The landing was in darkness, of course, but there was a two-way switch within her reach. Her extended finger shook, she stabbed twice at the small square of plastic. It clicked loudly.

But the upstairs light did not come on. The bulb must have blown.

Another smell assailed her nostrils, she did not recognize it. She coughed, it was unpleasant in a different sort of way, like . . . heated plastic. It seemed to be coming from the lounge.

Still there was no noise from the television. Perhaps there was a partial power failure that had affected the landing light and the television. First, though, she had to find out if there was an intruder in the house.

She could telephone for help, it didn't *have* to be the

police. Mr Morgan would come across, he wouldn't mind at all. Her shaking hand lifted the telephone, she was aware immediately that there was no dialling tone.

It wasn't working, either.

Betty Wilkins shuddered. She could always go across the street and fetch John Morgan. She hesitated, knew why she wouldn't go. Because it meant passing *his* house. That prospect was as fearsome as confronting a burglar. You had the feeling, day and night, that *he* was watching, lurking behind the curtains, observing everybody and everything. Watching and waiting.

For what?

Her foot rested on the bottom stair, her hand grasped the rail. The house had suddenly gone very cold, that strange smell was much stronger.

One step. Two. She did not bother calling out again because whoever it was would not answer her.

And then she saw him, a slip of a boy standing in the landing shadows; he was wearing some kind of nightshirt, a crumpled grubby gown that trailed around his bare feet. She couldn't see his face but there was something familiar about his posture. One of the local boys, doubtless. He was too slight for Rick Morgan, not tall enough for Tom. A juvenile burglar.

'What do you think you're doing in my house?' She tried to sound stern but it came out weak and nervous.

He was waving an arm, gesticulating wildly, pointing downstairs.

'No, I won't go away.' She experienced a surge of reassurance, he was obviously frightened of her. 'I've a good mind to call the police and have you taken away.' *Except that the telephone is out of order and by the time I've run to get Mr Morgan, you'll have fled.* 'Come on, show yourself properly, I want to see who you are!'

The boy seemed to be struggling, trying to obey but something was holding him back forcibly. Straining, breathing hard with the exertion, he was waving his arms again, desperately trying to convey something to her.

'You spoke before, why can't you now?'

She coughed, her eyes watered. That smell which she could not identify earlier, she knew what it was now. *It was smoke, something was burning in the front room.*

She half-turned back, and in that instant the stranger on the landing tore himself free of his invisible restraints; he staggered, almost fell, tottered unsteadily on the brink of the very top stair.

The light from the hallway fell on his face, and recognition was followed almost immediately by Betty Wilkins' hysterical scream.

No, it was impossible, as impossible as the return of Edward Kroll. For those boyish, anguished, dirt-smeared features belonged to none other than Mickey Farrell.

He was yelling but no sound came from his blistered lips, trying to warn her of something. He swayed, lost his balance, fell backwards. Like somebody in the darkness behind had grabbed him, dragged him away in case his warning was heeded.

Movement returned to Betty's legs, she knew that she had to flee this house before some dreadful catastrophe befell her. The warning had been frantic, unmistakable.

Go, before it is too late!

It was too late. From the front-room doorway thick black, pungent smoke was billowing, that suffocating stench of burning plastic which she had smelled before and failed to heed. It filled the hall, the heat that drove it was intense, seared her flesh.

Her escape route to the front door was blocked by that villainous cloud and the scorching heat. Her eyes watered, blurred her vision. She grasped the stair rail, tried to haul herself up.

Her strength was ebbing fast, breathing was becoming impossible as her lungs filled with smoke. The remainder of the power supply failed, everywhere was plunged into choking darkness.

Betty Wilkins felt consciousness slipping from her. Far away, in the depths of a smoke-filled abyss, she heard Mickey

Farrell screaming; not the warning which he had failed to voice earlier, instead it was a shriek of sheer terror as though his very soul was being tortured by the evil force he had defied in his futile attempt to save her.

Nineteen

'Well.' Christine Morgan stood by the rear kitchen door that led out on the snow covered yard, arms folded. 'You'd better go tell him, John. *Now*!'

John Morgan nodded, did not meet his wife's gaze. She was both angry and frightened, like the rest of this town. The snow made it worse, kind of trapped you in with your living nightmare. The road to Presteigne wasn't opened up yet, Rock Hill would be closed for a few more days, and the only means of travelling to Llandrindod Wells was by a 4x4 vehicle.

Christine's eyes were red-rimmed from sleeplessness. The fire tender had been parked outside for most of the night; the atmosphere had been acrid with pungent smoke from an electrical fire; it was probably Betty Wilkins's television that had set the place on fire.

The paramedics had stretchered somebody up to the waiting ambulance at the top of the Narrows. Everybody knew that the victim was Betty.

It had been announced on local radio this morning that she had died from smoke inhalation.

'You're not going to tell him, are you?' Christine whispered, afraid lest their only customer in the dining room might overhear. From where she stood she could hear Edward Kroll's noisy, revolting eating. Today was Tuesday, all-day breakfast day. He broke wind loudly, grunting his satisfaction.

'I don't know, I really don't.' John shrugged his shoulders helplessly. Those who offended their nemesis died a horrible death. John had long given up trying to explain the tragedies as coincidences.

'We can't go on like this, John.'

'Neither can the rest of the town. When I went down to Tuffins this morning there was a crowd gathered by the cenotaph, they were in an ugly mood. Scared and angry. I'm scared what it might lead to.'

'I'm not.' Her head jerked up, there was defiance in her expression. 'I don't care what they do so long as we're rid of him. The police aren't doing anything. Why don't they open up the grave, either confirm or destroy the rumours? At least that way we'd know the truth.'

'They can't do that without a licence from the Home Office and, cut off like we are now, London might as well be a million miles away. The idea would be laughed at up there; they might authorize a grave to be opened up as evidence in a murder enquiry but who, in their right mind, would believe in the walking dead? Except the townspeople of Knighton. The weather's an important factor, too, because the ground's rock hard, it would be impossible to carry out an exhumation. At the very earliest, they'd have to do it when the thaw came and the weathermen can't see any end to these arctic conditions.'

'I don't want him in here again.' Christine was sullen, defiant. 'I'll tell him myself if you're scared to.'

He stepped in her path, knew that she would have gone right through to the dining room and told Kroll what was on her mind.

'No!' John whispered. 'You know what happened to Betty, to the . . .'

'I'm doing it for the boys.' She was tense, fists bunched. 'I don't care what happens to me but Tom and Rick are going through hell. It might have serious consequences on their mental stability.'

'Or we might all be burned in our beds!'

He saw a new fear flicker in her eyes, a threat that went beyond her own safety. 'I might send Tom and Rick to my mother's for a while.'

'How? Ask the snowplough crews to drop them off at Llanddewi, cut a special path up there on their way home? Or wait for the thaw? *If* there's anything in these ridiculous stories about Kroll taking revenge on those who upset him, then he doesn't hang around. His vengeance is quick. You'll have to get the boys out of here today and, if you do, watch out for the snowploughs, he's got some control over them!'

'Bastard!'

John didn't know whether she meant himself or Kroll.

'We can't go on, John.' She was close to breaking point. Like the guys who had gathered down by the war memorial this morning. It was just a question of who broke first.

'*Pudding*!'

The shrill cry of aggrieved impatience from the adjoining room jerked them back to their immediate predicament. Christine recoiled, for a moment John thought that she was going to rush outside through the back door; run and keep on running.

'I'll see to it.' He pulled himself together, went through to the dining area.

'I've been waiting for over five minutes!' Edward Kroll checked the wristwatch that hung loosely on his thin wrist.

'I'm sorry, we were discussing tomorrow's menu.' His lower lip trembled, the lie came falteringly.

'I don't come here on Wednesdays.'

'No, of course not.'

The Tupperware box had condensed from the heat of its contents. Egg yolk was congealing on Kroll's lips, he had dropped some on his lapels. 'I'll have the trifle today.'

'I'm sorry, the trifle's all gone. There's apple and blackberry pie . . .'

'And full of pips!' He spat at the thought. 'Why don't you make more trifle?'

'You've never asked for trifle before.'

'It's on the board!' A finger stabbed its accusation at the 'specials' blackboard on the wall. 'Did it not occur to you to erase it and thereby not disappoint customers who were tempted by it?'

'I haven't had time.'

'There's been nobody else in here this morning apart

from those two gossipy women who come for their insipid cups of tea each day!'

Damn him, he'd been spying from behind his curtains, he probably sat there all day. And night.

'We have a lot of preparation and cleaning to do. The health inspectors are very strict, they make unscheduled calls. We pride ourselves in—'

'I'll have apple pie and custard.'

'Very good.' Oh, God, he knew he'd lost his nerve, because Kroll was even more ill-tempered than usual, aggressive. 'Oh, there's something I want to speak to you about, Mr Kroll.' If he didn't do it, Christine would.

'About the broken window, and about time too!'

'Actually, no . . .'

'Actually, *yes*! The damage must be paid for.'

'I understand that it was young Wyke who is supposed to have smashed your window with an airgun pellet. Sadly, Steve is dead.'

'The weapon came from here, was lent to him for a nefarious purpose. Consequently, as a parent, you must take responsibility for your sons' foolishness. Had they not lent the gun to the miscreant, my window would still be intact.'

John Morgan felt himself go cold all over. 'I really don't think that you have any claim upon me or my sons, Mr Kroll.'

'*I* do. The room inside that particular window has been dirtied by the smoke from last night's fire. Some of the books will need professional cleaning and that is an expensive process. The blame must be laid on yourself, for had the window not been smashed then the smoke would not have infiltrated. Do I make myself clear?'

'I think you will find, Mr Kroll, upon consulting your lawyer, that you can claim for damages against the owner of the property that was on fire. Or her estate. Miss Wilkins died in the fire.'

'But the window still must be paid for!' He banged a puny fist on the table, rattling the knife and fork on his empty plate. His features were a terrifying mask of childish petulance. '*You will pay for it*!' The shriek rose to a crescendo, died away.

'I was about to say,' John's countered as his anger overcame his fear, 'that, as from tonight, we are closing the Grillhouse for a while . . .'

'Are you going to pay for the repair of the window or not? I must know.'

Jesus Almighty! John was sweating, somehow he managed to check his rising anger. 'I am trying to tell you that this restaurant won't be open after today.'

There was a sudden silence. Kroll's mouth pouted, twitched like he was still masticating his midday breakfast, preparing to spit out a particle of indigestible bacon gristle. 'You mean . . . it will be *closed*?'

'Exactly.'

'I shall require sustenance on Thursday. Cottage pie, as usual. Perhaps you will be kind enough to cook some for me even though you will not be open to the general public.'

Oh, God! 'We plan to take a short winter break, Mr Kroll.'

'But you won't be vacating the premises, there is nowhere to go, is there, at this time of year? I understand that the town is virtually cut off by the snow drifts. All I ask is that you prepare a meal for me at precisely one forty on Thursday, and again the following Tuesday, a week today. Doubtless you are planning a quiet family rest together but you will still have to cook for yourselves. One extra meal will not inconvenience you, I am sure.'

'We had hoped to go away.'

'But now you cannot.' There was no mistaking the chilling implication. 'And, returning to the question of the broken window for which I have to be reimbursed, perhaps you would prefer to pay me in kind?'

'I . . . I'm afraid I don't understand you, Mr Kroll.'

'You seem to have difficulty in grasping the simplest of bargains.' He gestured his impatience as his fist threatened to bang the table again. 'Instead of paying me in cash, you pay me in meals. Now, let me see . . .' He counted on his skeletal fingers, bent his head in deep concentration. 'A replacement pane of glass, including labour at an extortionate charge, would amount to something in the region of twenty pounds, I am sure. I will be generous and allow you two pounds, fifty pence per serving of main course and dessert and a cup of your insipid tea. Yes –' his head jerked up, a finger was raised, the lips parted in a mirthless smile – 'eight meals should suffice. Today, I will pay cash but as from Thursday, and for the four weeks following that, I shall eat here free of charge. In cash terms, I mean. Now, Mr Morgan, do I make myself clear?'

John found himself nodding, he was totally confused. And frightened. That momentary inspiration, a compromise with Chrissie's demand to be rid of Kroll by closing the Grillhouse, was suddenly dashed.

'Apple pie!' Edward Kroll waved for him to remove the greasy plate and return to the kitchen. 'With custard, thick and yellow, not watery and pallid like it was last week.'

John was shaking as he returned to the kitchen. Christine was busying herself wiping down the working surfaces; her back was towards him but he could tell that she was sobbing.

He had tried and failed. They were not even going to be allowed a temporary respite from Edward Kroll.

Outside, the sky had clouded over. It was starting to snow again.

Twenty

Voices carried in the building that had once been a fifteenth-century brothel and was now the Grillhouse; especially whispers. It was as though a host of phantom listeners that dwelled therein mimicked the words of the living, passed them from one to another, all the way up the winding staircase to the first landing, transmitted them up to the attic which was now Rick and Tom's bedroom.

The boys had listened to the conversations downstairs, both in the kitchen and the dining area. They had eavesdropped with macabre fascination, their PlayStation forgotten. Crouched in the attic doorway, they trembled in a continuation of the previous night's terror.

Throughout the nocturnal hours they had stood shivering in the cold, their faces pressed against the window, watched the fire crew battling with the flames in the ground floor rooms of Betty Wilkins' house.

They had seen the lifeless shape, enshrouded in blankets, stretchered away. They knew why she had died, just as they knew the reasons for all the other deaths. And their greatest fear now was that Kroll was blaming them for having lent the airgun to Steve Wyke.

The slamming of the outer door as Kroll left the restaurant was but a temporary relief because they knew that he would be back. His return would be even worse if their parents closed the restaurant because they would be trapped in here with him.

'The school will stay closed till the snow thaws,' Tom said and voiced what they had both been thinking, that there would be no respite from this twice-weekly routine. 'There's nowhere else to go 'cept down the street.'

'It's snowing again.'

'That means it's turned warmer, there'll be a thaw.'

'You're kiddin'. It'll lie on top of what's already fallen. It'll take weeks to melt, then the pipes will probably burst in the school and they'll keep it closed even longer.'

'*He* burned old Bet, you know that.' Rick was shaking. 'Like he pushed Mickey under that van, cut Steve's throat and chucked him down a mine shaft, gave the bookman a heart attack, cut off the council man's head and—'

'*Shaddup*!' Tom's half scream was strangled by a choking sob.

'Well, it's true, no good trying to find other reasons.'

'Prove it!'

'Don't need to, you can ask anybody in town, everybody says the same. Now he's saying it's *our* fault his fucking window got broke. And don't start crying because it won't do no good, it won't change nothin'.'

'Maybe we should run away. We could go to Aunt Ivy's in Presteigne.'

'And end up in a snowdrift with our throats slit. Or maybe just freeze to death out there. Tom, we gotta *do* something.'

'Oh, yeah! What?'

'I've been thinking.'

'Makes a change.'

'You remember when Uncle Arthur died?'

'Sort of. They wouldn't let me go to the funeral, said I was too young. I 'ad to stay with old Bet, she brought me home from school, stayed with me until everybody got home.'

'Well, *I* went. They didn't bury him although the funeral was in town. We had to go all the way to Hereford to 'ave 'im cremated.'

'Oh, I see.' Tom wasn't really interested, it had to be five or six years ago. Aunt Ivy lived on her own now, had stayed on in the same house in Presteigne.

'Cremations are much better than burials. I mean, what use is a corpse to anybody? Might as well burn it as take up ground with graves.'

Tom shivered. He didn't want to discuss funerals.

'Don't you think,' Rick said as he lowered his voice, 'that if they'd cremated *him*, then all this wouldn't've happened. I mean, they'd've burned 'im, there wouldn't be anythin' left to come back, would there?'

The other caught his breath. 'I see what you mean. But it's too late now, isn't it?'

'Is it?'

'What . . . what d'you mean?' Tom swallowed.

'Kroll's dead, ain't he? Everybody says so, so it's gotta be right. So, if he was burned, it would only be like cremating him, not murder or anything like that.'

'Rick, *no*!'

'Why not?

'We'd go to prison . . . or else *he'd* do something awful to us.'

'No,' Rick Morgan said with a smile, trying to appear confident.

'We won't go to prison because we're too young. At the very worst we'd get community service but we won't even get that because nobody will know. And Kroll will be roasted like a scraggy old chicken before he gets time to do anything to us. See?'

'It's risky.' Tom's guts had balled and he felt slightly sick. 'Sounds too easy.'

'It is easy.' Rick felt more confident now that he had put his idea into words. 'Dad keeps a spare can of petrol in the garage in case he ever needs it. All we need to do is to creep out after dark, we'll go through the yard and into Kroll's that way. Chuck some into his kitchen and all it needs is one match. *Whoosh* and we're away. We'll be back up here before anybody knows we've been gone. We can rush downstairs to ask what's going on when the fire tender gets here.'

'I still don't like it, Rick.'

'Well, you don't have to bloody come with me, I'll go alone and you can swear blind that I was upstairs with you all evening. We'll wait till *Casualty* starts on the telly, nothing'll drag Mum and Dad away from that, they even put the answerphone on while they watch it.'

It sounded good. Too good. Tom began to tremble. Everybody could be rid of Edward Kroll for good. 'Suppose the fire spreads to this place, it's only three doors away?' That was something else to worry about.

'No chance.' Rick wasn't going to consider obstacles, his mind was made up. 'Remember how quick they got Betty Wilkins's fire out? There may be a bit of damage to the houses on either side but we can't help that. Jesus, anything's worth ridding the town of *him*. Folks'll be able to sleep easy at nights then.'

'I guess you're right,' Tom acknowledged with a nod. 'I'll come with you.'

'Good, but we'll have to get the timing right. Let *Casualty* get started. If we go from here at five past nine, we'll be back by ten past. You can reckon the alarm won't be raised for another five or ten minutes after that. Jesus Christ, Edward Kroll's in for a warm time, I'll promise you that!'

This time they both laughed.

'Where are you going, Chad?' There was alarm in Lindy Lloyd's voice.

'Just out.' His reply was evasive, he didn't meet her searching gaze. 'I might pop up to the Lion or the George for a drink.'

'Then I'll come with you, we haven't been out for ages.' And nobody goes out alone these nights, if at all.

'I was hoping I might do some business.'

'What kind of business?'

'A story, maybe. Christ, there hasn't been any football for three weeks now, freelancing isn't easy, you know.'

'What *kind* of a story. Not . . . not *him*?'

'Perhaps.'

'*No*!' She stepped forward as though to bar his way. 'Not after last time. Oh, God, I thought I was going mad and you still haven't told me what really happened.'

'Maybe I'll pick up some material in the pubs, everybody's got a story about "him" as you say.'

'But you know damned well nobody will publish it, a

combination of fear of libel and what might happen to them if they did.'

'A lot's happened since then, love.'

'Sure, three people have died in mysterious and horrible circumstances. You were lucky, Chad.' Lindy was white and shaking. 'Please, don't stir up anything else.'

'All I'm looking for –' he drew her to him, kissed her – 'is a different angle on things, maybe somebody who was at the fire. You don't know in this job until you get out there and talk to people.'

'I wish you wouldn't.' She held him close.

'Look, it's just after eight now. I promise I'll be back by ten, ten thirty at the latest. How's that?'

'I suppose so.' She extricated herself. If Chad was going out looking for a story then she knew she would not be welcome. People were less likely to talk to him when she was around. 'But if you're not back by ten, I'll be phoning round the pubs for you.'

'It's a deal.' He stepped out on to the landing, closing the door behind him.

The night was starry and bitterly cold, the frozen snow crunched beneath his feet. There had been a snow shower earlier in the day but it had passed on. The forecast was for temperatures around minus ten again tonight. He pushed his hands deep into his pockets.

No way was he going inside Kroll's house again but he would most certainly take a look from the outside. Had that broken window been mended? Maybe there would be a light in one of the windows, a shadow on the curtain. Even that had him shuddering. He might just knock the door on the remote chance that it would be answered.

In all probability, he wouldn't do anything more than observe from a distance.

The lounge bar of the George & Dragon was unaccustomedly crowded for a weeknight. The stag's head on the wall peered out from a haze of tobacco smoke, antique mugs hung from the oaken beams. Larry had his customary stool at the far end of the polished bar and regarded the gathering with an expression of disapproval. He knew that everybody had turned out for the same reason that he had, the need for company, safety in numbers. Things were bad, they might get worse.

Victor Pohl was extolling the virtues of craftsmanmade coffins; nobody was interested. He had made Kroll's coffin, nobody could have got out of that, he'd screwed it down personally. All the same, there was no explanation for what had happened in the mortuary that night and for that reason he had not told anybody. They would put it down to drink or senility, or a combination of both. All the same, his own experience wasn't as far-fetched as some of the things that had gone on in town since Kroll's burial.

The grave hadn't been touched, Victor had been down to look that morning. A mound of earth covered with snow and frozen solid. It would take a mechanical digger to shift that lot. There had to be some explanation that nobody had thought of.

That police officer's visit had unnerved Victor. Bloody crazy! They'd lost the death certificate, now they were seeking reassurance that Kroll was actually dead! Well, there had been that instance a few years back when they'd brought Mrs Potter in and Victor had commenced the task of laying her out. She'd had a long illness, cancer, and had been in the cottage hospital for weeks. Suddenly, she'd stirred on the slab and started to moan; they'd taken her back to hospital and she'd lingered another three days. Which just went to show that even the medical profession made mistakes sometimes.

Doc King had popped round yesterday, too. He didn't ask outright in his usual abrupt manner if the old bugger was dead, but pertinent questions led Victor to believe that the medic was having second thoughts. It had been King who had made a mistake over Mrs Potter, he was obviously having his doubts about Kroll now.

All of which gave you the shivers, even when you handled corpses regularly. The dead were fine, it was the living you had to watch out for. Victor sipped his beer meditatively. Business had been good lately. Too good for comfort if you stopped to think about it.

He noticed the huddle in the far corner, faces he knew: Reuben Wilson, Jack Loiney, Alan Fairclough, a couple of others that he could not put names to. Council workers whose main task these last few weeks had been to keep the streets around town clear of snow. A bloody disagreeable lot, made out they were doing everybody a favour. They forgot that the townspeople paid their wages. Victor remembered the time, a few years back, when they'd gone on strike, some disagreement over the length of tea breaks. Reuben had started it all, he was a big union man and always looking for a dispute with his employers. The conflict had escalated, spread to other departments. Garbage wasn't collected for a fortnight, even the recreation parks' gardeners had downed tools.

In the end, Reuben won; tea breaks were extended by five minutes and the workers received a rise in wages. Bloody disgraceful, it was, and judging by the expression on Reuben's face right now he was stirring up more trouble. Their heads were bent forward in deep conversation, they had obviously come to the George for an unofficial union meeting in preparation for some grievance which they would be lodging with their employers tomorrow.

Victor turned his back on them in disgust.

'We gotta fix 'im,' Reuben Wilson whispered throatily, lit another cigarette and held it in a cupped hand. 'No two ways about it, none of us are safe and the law won't do nothin' about it. That blade chopped Dai's head straight off and the maintenance inspector says that there's nothing wrong with the mechanism. It should've come down nice and slow, he'd've had plenty o' time to get from under it. Accident, my ass! And the old biddy who reported Kroll got killed in a fire hours afterwards. Is that a coincidence?'

'No way!' Jack Loiney narrowed his resentful eyes. 'You're right, Reuben, question is, 'ow far do we go?'

'The whole bleedin' hog!' An even lower whisper. 'The bugger's dead, he has to be, and if he isn't –' he drew hard on his cigarette, let the smoke out slowly – 'he bloody soon will be!'

Alan Fairclough paled, looked at the other two. They nodded slowly. 'Reuben's right.' Gerald Crofts was related to Fred Tricklebank by marriage, he'd heard the full story, in detail, from his brother-in-law. 'We gotta do it. Nobody'll know, provided we're careful.'

'It's him or us.' Wilson's eyes roved around the circle of companions, settling on each one in turn. 'We're all in it together. Not that it'll ever come to that,' he said with a laugh and checked his pocket watch. 'Time now is twenty minutes to nine. There's a can of petrol in the back of the truck. Drink up, leave one at a time and meet down the Cwm in a quarter of an hour. Guy Fawkes night will 'ave nothing on tonight, the biggest blaze you'll ever see with a real live Guy on the top of the bonfire!'

They drained their glasses, Reuben Wilson left first, followed by Jack Loiney.

Chad had watched from across the room. There was nothing unusual in a gang of council workmen meeting up to discuss their grievances over a pint of ale. Neither was there anything unduly suspicious in a whispered conversation. It was their expressions, their furtiveness, that alerted a gut feeling that had stood him in good stead in the past. A hunch was always worth following, especially when there was nothing else doing.

Chad followed on the heels of Alan Fairclough and kept to the shadows.

'Time we weren't here.' Rick Morgan stood up. The last computer game had been a farce, neither of them had been concentrating.

They left the demo on, to have switched off the set might have aroused suspicion had either of their parents checked on them in their absence. They wouldn't, though, not when *Casualty* was showing.

The stairs creaked, there was no way of stopping them, but it didn't matter. Rick and Tom often went down for refreshment in between games. The door through to the yard had iced up, they had to force it open; it made a cracking sound.

'Maybe we shouldn't . . .' Tom slid on the frozen yard, then regained his balance.

'Fuck off, go back if you want!' Rick was headed towards the garage. The petrol can was kept just inside the door; he had checked on it earlier.

Tom waited; even in his T-shirt and jeans he did not notice the cold. He saw that Rick had the can, heard the contents slopping about. It was too late to chicken out now.

The usually muddy track that served the rear of the Narrows was hard and uncomfortable to sneakered feet. If you didn't trip over a rut, you might slip on patches of ice where the puddles had long frozen. Rick was in the lead, hugging the deep shadows cast by leaning fences and straggling, snow-laden hedges. Here and there a window was lit up, the houses were mostly in darkness.

'That's *his* back gate.'

'Shaddup!'

'Rick . . . listen!' Tom plucked at his brother's sweatshirt.

'Jesus, I told you to—'

'I can hear something!'

Rick checked his 'fuck off' reply and listened. It was nothing, Tom was shitting his jeans, he'd imagine all sorts of things. 'It's nothing . . .'

It was something. A noise that sounded like this afternoon's snowfall being compressed into the packed snow that already lay on the ground; a crispy crunching that stopped, began again. Stopped.

'There's somebody coming,' Tom mouthed not daring even to whisper it. There was still time to run, put the petrol can back in the garage and return to their game. That way they would have done nothing wrong, it would all have been a game of fantasy.

'They're coming from the other direction.' Rick turned, cupped his hand to whisper in Tom's ear. 'Get under the hedge, they won't see us.'

It was cold and wet and scary beneath the snow-weighted privet branches. A lump of frozen snow dropped inside Tom's shirt, almost had him crying out loud. More stealthy footsteps; there was more than one person headed this way.

A sound of breathing, a heavy cigarette smoker taking icy air down into his nicotine-coated lungs; trying not to cough, a sort of retching sound. The footfalls ceased, somebody was whispering.

Rick peered out cautiously from their hiding place, Tom heard his brother's sharp intake of breath.

'What is it?'

Rick did not answwser. In the half light, the reflection from the snow and the distant street lighting, he made out a huddle of figures. He counted them; four, at least, maybe five. They, too, were pressed back against the leaning fence that marked the extremity of Edward Kroll's back yard.

It might have been a group of drinkers returning home, perhaps relieving themselves after an excess of ale; their furtiveness might have been due to their fear of being surprised in the act of urinating in a public place. But Rick sensed that it was neither of these that had them whispering, and the slopping sound that came from a cannister held by one of them was most certainly not a flagon of beer being carried for consumption at home.

It wasn't too late to retreat. If the others had heard them, then they would not have recognized them. And, anyway, so far no crime had been committed. Rick twisted himself around, whispered, 'We'd better leave it for now. Maybe try again tomorrow. Head back as quietly as you can . . .'

It was already too late. Even as Tom shifted position, he was aware of more footfalls, slow stealthy ones as if whoever it was tested the ground in front before lowering his weight on it. A glimpse of a shadowy shape before it ducked under a low hanging elder branch and was swallowed up by the shadows.

'Shitfire!' Rick breathed his fear and frustration into his companion's face. 'The fucker's behind us, there's no way back!'

The silence was terrifying. The Morgans pressed themselves deeper into the hedge; maybe they had not been seen either by those in front or whoever it was behind them. If they kept still maybe everybody would go their separate ways.

Nobody moved. It was as if everybody was watching and waiting for something to happen.

Rick and Tom began to shiver, they heard their teeth

chattering with cold and fear. Minutes seemed like hours; surely *Casualty* was finished by now and the Morgans would have missed their sons. Maybe that was Dad back there, he had heared them leave and had followed them. Or the police had guessed that somebody might get the notion to burn Kroll's house down.

Or maybe it was Kroll himself, waiting out here to trap them, to exact his terrible vengeance on the owners of the airgun that had broken his window.

Tom was sobbing, whoever was out there in the freezing night must surely hear him. Rick slid the petrol can through the hedge, they must not be caught in possession of it. Maybe if they just walked out from the hedge, pretended they were on their way home, nobody would suspect. Kids always *used* to roam the streets after dark.

He started to straighten up and that was when the explosion fired the night sky with a column of orange flame. It came from close by, they felt its scorching heat, a slumbering dragon that had been disturbed and vented its fiery fury upon those who had trespassed too close.

Edward Kroll's house was illuminated in its dilapidation, flames leaping high and adhering to the brittle woodwork, securing a hold on window frames, crackling on dry kindling. The flames hissed on ivy, shrivelling it in its wake, leaping on until they found another hold; spreading horizontally and vertically. It was a raging furnace that showered sparks, roared its greed as glass panes cracked and shards tinkled on the yard below.

Rick and Tom were frozen into immobility. They heard voices, cursings, heavy footfalls that were no longer stealthy, slipping and crunching on the frozen roadway. Fleeing.

Behind them that shadowy shape had emerged from beneath the elder tree, ran and turned back to watch. If they were seen, they would be blamed for what others had done; the hidden can of petrol would be proof of their guilt.

Somebody else was coming, fast light footfalls from the direction in which those men had retreated. No, not quite, the footsteps came from down the yard which adjoined the house that had become an inferno.

The boys heard the click of the latch on the gate, it sagged on its broken hinges. A silhouette, slight and boyish, it paused as though it was uncertain in which direction to go.

It made a decision, turned towards where Rick and Tom crouched in hiding. And that was when the fiery glow fell full upon it and revealed its features in every detail.

Boyish and yet more terrible to behold than even Edward Kroll's cadaverous countenance. A final glance before it fled, passed so close to the cowering Morgans that there could be no possible mistake in identification. Even the expression of hellish fury, as it turned to gloat over the column of fire that climbed even higher into the night sky, could not disguise features that were so familiar to both watchers.

The watchers screamed, clung to each other. The raging fire, the unknown lurkers who had fled this dreadful place, all else was forgotten. Their minds tottered on the narrow brink that separated sanity from madness as they struggled to believe that which their eyes had seen. Impossibility became terrible reality.

For he who had run from those flames, which surely spouted up from hell itself, was none other than Mickey Farrell.

Twenty-One

Chad grabbed Lindy in an attempt to stop her from screaming hysterically, he shook her roughly when his reassurances failed to quieten her. He might even have hit her had she not suddenly calmed. That would have plagued his conscience for ever; the lowest bastard of all was the one who struck a woman, whatever the reason.

'I'm *all right*.' He pulled her close, held her to him. 'I'm OK.'

'You've been inside . . . *his* house again!' She spat out the accusation. 'Oh, God, just look at you, I know you have. Just like last time!'

'I swear to God I haven't.' He stiffened suddenly. 'Listen!'

They heard the wailing of a fire engine down in the street below, a banshee deafening them with its premonition of death. Death had already come to Knighton and it would surely return before this night was out. Then a high pitched whining as a police car followed in the wake of the tender; the ambulance would not be far behind, a cacophony of noise that heralded yet another tragedy for this accursed town.

'Kroll's house is on fire.' He tried to speak calmly. 'By morning, unless I'm very much mistaken, neither it nor he will exist. It's an inferno.'

She dragged herself free of his embrace, stared aghast at him. 'Oh, no! Chad, *no*! You're as bad as him, it's like some mediaeval nightmare, a witchfinder burning him at the stake to appease the superstitious locals!'

'I didn't start the fire, I promise you that, Lindy.' He found a pack of cigarettes, lit one. If this was a nightmare, he prayed that he would wake up soon.

'Who did, then?'

'I wish I knew. I followed a bunch of guys out of the pub. I'm certain that their intention was to torch the house but they didn't get close enough. There were a couple of kids crouched under a hedge but it wasn't them, either. Then somebody ran away from the fire, I didn't get a good look at him. Just another kid, as far as I could make out. Maybe it was him who started the fire.'

'They'll think it was you that did it, Chad,' she said and buried her face against him. 'Oh, God, if only you hadn't gone out tonight.'

'I'm certain nobody saw me after I left the George.' He drew deeply on his cigarette. 'You're right, Lindy, it was just like something out of the Middle Ages, the townsfolk setting out after dark to destroy the witch that has plagued them for so long. Scared to hell, safety in numbers, and even then they only found their courage in drink. And then somebody goes and beats them to it!' He laughed, it was a chilling sound.

Outside, the night was filled with blaring sirens, flashing blue lights penetrated the curtains, flickered on the walls. Chad's nostrils flared, you could smell the smoke now.

Crowds thronged both ends of the Narrows, faces bathed in the smoky orange glow from the fire; frightened expressions that seemed to be hypnotized by the flames. Huddling, watching. Waiting.

Burn the Undead! Let us be rid of him for ever!

Sergeant Davison and PC Morris had evacuated all the houses in close proximity; the blaze might spread, take the entire row right down to the clocktower. Timbers cracked, sparks showered high into the sky in an aurora borealis of evil.

The glass was gone from the windows; it littered the streets, left gaping eyes that blazed hatred, not just on the one who had dared to commit arson but on the entire townspeople. Because they willed Edward Kroll and his dark lair to be reduced to a pile of ashes.

The Morgans watched from a distance, held their sons

to them as they had not done since Rick and Tom were infants. John had been the first to notice the fire, *Casualty* was abandoned, it was now for real. Their home, their livelihood was threatened.

'It'll burn the houses either side,' Christine shouted, trying to make herself heard above the crackling and hissing. 'We're two doors down, we might be all right if they can contain it.'

John nodded. They were helpless, pawns of fate. 'He probably went to sleep smoking a cigarette.' He didn't have to look for a cause but he wanted it to be an accident. Kroll's vengeance was too terrible to contemplate, he might punish them all for this.

Water gushed down the snow packed street, by morning huge pools of it would be frozen around the clocktower and down Broad Street.

'The roof's collapsing!' A shriek from the crowd was followed by a slippery retreat.

The roof caved inwards, avalanched down into the depths of the inferno, shuddered the ground like an earthquake. The fire crew stood back, continued to play their hoses on the flames. Another tender battled from the rear of the Narrows, soaking the adjacent property in foam in the hope that the fire would not spread.

'It ain't spreading.' A fireman turned to shout back to his chief. 'It's almost like it's just going to burn itself out in there!'

'Can't take any chances.' The chief had fought more fires than any of his men, it would be a miracle if the houses on either side didn't catch. 'Keep it up, we can't do any more.'

Flaked paper was floating up out of the fiery shell as the books burned, drifting over the town, settling on buildings. Where previously there had been a virgin whiteness now there was blackness. Edward Kroll had forced the town into mourning.

The new day dawned grey and smoky, the air was heavy with the smell of burning. Only the stone walls of the gutted house remained, an old-fashioned oven that had cooked its roast to a cinder. Wisping smoke from the deep embers that hissed their protest at the incessant jets of water, ashes that were a metre deep on the ground floor.

The fire had been controlled; miraculously, the other houses had suffered no more than heat scorching and smoke damage.

With the coming of daylight the crowds drifted away. Their relief was evident, nothing could have survived in that inferno, neither the living nor the dead.

The police forensic team worked tirelessly throughout the following day. Clad in protective gear, they raked and probed through the debris, the slightest movement sent up clouds of fine ash dust. Passers-by glanced curiously over the red and white rope cordon, peered through the gutted doorway and lower windows. Sinister shapes moved, goggle-eyed creatures that might have come from outer space.

The search was twofold; there was as much chance of finding the remains of a body as there would have been in a crematorium, so samples of ash were collected in special containers to be removed for laboratory tests; likewise, the cause of the fire needed to be ascertained. Accident or arson? After a blaze of this intensity the latter would be difficult to determine. But they would be able to tell whether or not a human body had been consumed in the inferno.

Meanwhile, the townspeople waited anxiously. So long as Edward Kroll was gone from their midst, nothing else mattered. If the fire had been started deliberately then may God's blessing be upon the arsonist. The following Sunday they prayed silently, almost guiltily, in church and chapel that their saviour might be forgiven and protected from the police.

Detective Inspector Ian Glanville had supervised the meticulous search of the burned out house. A typically no-nonsense CID officer in his mid-thirties, his lived-in features wore an expression that was inscrutable even to his close colleagues. His ambition was to make it to Chief Inspector. Such cases as this were a challenge, a possible notch nearer his goal. Unless, of course, the fire was accidental. He would move heaven and earth and a ton of ashes to prove that it was not.

'Anything?' He stood in the blackened doorway, watching as the three officers removed masks and goggles.

'Nothing to speak of.' The nearest officer was sweating badly.

'Bloody books, must have been more in this house than in the library, all charred to a mountain of ash. That's virtually all that was in the place apart from a few odds and ends. We've enough here –' he indicated a row of polythene containers – 'to keep the lab busy for a month!'

'The fire started at the back.' Glanville was talking for his own benefit, trying to put the events into chronological order just in case he'd missed anything. 'According to the fire chief and the insurance assessor, it began in the kitchen area, maybe even the back door, swept upwards then on into the house.'

'So if anybody had had enough warning they could've got out the front?'

'Possibly, although the staircase might have been smoke-filled so that they couldn't get down. Unless, of course, they happened to be downstairs at the front of the house.'

'My guess is, sir, they'll find human ash in this lot. If the occupant had escaped, he'd've raised the alarm himself, wouldn't he?'

'Perhaps.' Glanville had heard the stories about Kroll but the detective was only interested in facts. This whole business reeked of some kind of insurance fraud. It was going to be difficult to prove. 'The other alternative is that he wasn't at home when the fire broke out.'

That was Knighton's lingering fear, too, that Edward Kroll would return and take his revenge upon them because somebody had destroyed his home.

'I'm still waiting to hear.' George Edmonds' chair creaked as he leaned back. 'The police at Llandod promised that they'd let me know as soon as the lab have finished analysing innumerable samples of ash. God dammit, I *have* to know, is he dead or isn't he? There's a matter of probate that may linger on for years, a fire insurance that has to be paid out to somebody. Do we authorize rebuilding or wait, pending him turning up like he did before? This whole business is crazy.'

'Well, he was dead when I signed the certificate.' Dr King might have seemed a trifle uncertain of himself to anybody who knew him well enough. 'If somebody was passing himself off as Edward Kroll, then if he was in that house, they'll find his ashes. If they don't find anything, then he'd left before the fire started.'

'It's sod's law from start to finish,' the lawyer said as he shuffled some papers in a wire basket. 'If he'd died a week later, both the original and the copy death certificate would still be in the registrar's office. They send them to London quarterly. Kroll's went almost immediately because it fell just inside the last period. I've checked with London, the others have arrived, Kroll's went missing, presumably lost before they gave it a reference number and put it on microfiche. A chance in a million, but it's happened. It may turn up, they're searching frantically now to try to save themselves embarrassment. And there's another worrying factor . . .'

'Yes?'

'They can't find any trace of his birth certificate, either!'

The doctor froze in the act of filling his pipe. It might have been an illusion caused by the flickering of the fluorescent light but Edmonds thought that the medic's hands trembled.

'The incompetence of bureaucracy beggars belief.' King struck a match, the fingers that held it were rock steady now. 'Well, I'd better be getting back . . .'

The telephone on the desk rang, an outdated appliance that shrilled, vibrated its cracked and stained casing. Both men stared at it, it was like some squat creature shrieking at them. There was almost a premonition in its tone, a defiance even; *listen to me, if you dare*. It boded ill, the lawyer's outstretched hand hesitated.

Answer the bloody thing, King's expression said as he rose to his feet, perhaps a sudden urge to be away before bad news came through. It wasn't any of his business, anyway, he was a doctor.

Edmonds grunted into the mouthpiece, listened. A distant tinny voice, audible but incoherent to the reluctant eavesdropper.

'I see.' Edmonds' tone was flat, conveyed nothing. He had swivelled round so that his companion would be unable to read his expression. 'Thanks for letting me know. Keep me posted, please, if anything crops up.'

The receiver tinged mockingly as it was replaced, it had done its worst.

'That's that, then.' The lawyer turned back slowly, his features were ashen.

King waited, the other would tell him in his own good time.

'There is no evidence to suggest that the fire was deliberately started. It *could* have been a faulty kitchen appliance. The police are keeping the file open. Which means that they won't investigate further unless anything else occurs.'

King waited, knew the form. That's the bad news, now for the *very* bad news.

'They've completed their tests on the ashes,' Edmonds said slowly, deliberately. 'There is no trace of any human having been consumed by the flames!'

Twenty-Two

'I d'ain't much care for this lark!' Larry straightened up, leaning his sparse frame on the heavy shovel and tugging his cap down even more tightly as if to hide his features from the light of the half moon. 'In fact, I d'ain't like it at all! I shouldn't've come, I wouldn't've done if it wasn't for that last whisky you bought me when I said I didn'a want no more. I must be mad. Or bloomin' drunk.'

'You came because you know as well as I do that it's the only way.' Chad did his best to grin; standing in a partly opened grave, surrounded by rows of tombstones, in the early hours of the morning did not inspire a sense of humour. 'I don't like it any more than you do, Larry, but it has to be done. We *have* to find out, not just for ourselves but for the sake of everybody else in Knighton and the surrounding area.'

'Aye, but I'll guarantee that there's not one o' them that'll put up bail for us when we go to jail. They're too bloomin' mean!' He laughed throatily.

'Nobody will know.' Chad wished that he felt as confident as he tried to sound. 'The grave will be filled in again before dark and none one will even guess it's been tampered with.'

'I wouldn't count on it. There's not much happens round here that folks don't get to find out.'

Chad clattered another shovelful of stones and soil on to the growing heap by the graveside. 'Damned good job that the thaw came as soon and as fast as it did otherwise we might've had to wait until Spring to find out whether or not Kroll's still in his grave.'

The thaw had arrived a week to the day after Kroll's

house had been burned down, took the weather forecasters by surprise. An area of low pressure was sweeping in from the Atlantic, they predicted yet more blizzards. Then, without warning, the temperature rose and, instead of snow, torrential rain fell for forty-eight hours without a break. The hard ground was unable to soak up the deluge, most of the low lying ground was flooded as streams and rivers burst their banks. Ice and snow melted as the temperatures rose from minus six to fourteen.

The shovel squelched, there was mud where water had seeped down into the grave.

'I know why you're doing this!' Larry stopped suddenly as a thought occurred to him and he turned back to his companion, leaning across the rectangular hole, head thrust forward belligerently.

'Why's that?' Chad was standing in the grave, soon the work would become arduous as each shovelful would have to be lifted out of the cramped excavation.

'To write one of them there stories of yours about it for the paper!'

'I might even do that one day but I can assure you that is not my main reason for digging up the dead.'

'Then we'll both go to jail for sure.'

'It all depends on what we find down here.' Chad did not relish the prospect of opening up the coffin. Maybe, provided the lid was screwed down firmly, there was no reason to because the corpse would still be inside it. All the same, he'd take a look to satisfy himself, particularly after all this work.

Larry returned to his task. Soon there would only be room enough for them to work separately, they'd probably take the digging in turns. Chad did not really need the other's help, he had only persuaded him to come along because he was too damned scared to exhume the body on his own.

Larry had always boasted that he had no fear of Edward Kroll. 'If the blighter's dead, there's no way he can hurt you.' Which was logical. 'And if he ain't dead, then he hasn't got the strength to knock the skin off a rice pudding. So, either way, there's no point being scared of him.'

Chad wished that he could have shared Larry's philosophy. He might have done so had it not been for recent happenings. Dead or alive, weak as a child, Kroll still managed to burn folks in their houses, push them under vehicles or drop them down mineshafts, even behead them. According to superstitious gossip. Chad had been lucky. So far.

'It said in the paper that nobody had been burned in the fire.' Larry was tiring, using conversation as an excuse to rest and hoped that it would go unnoticed.

'You don't want to believe everything that you read in the newspapers.'

'You write the bloomin' stuff!'

'I cover sport.'

'Funny kinda sport.' The old man peered down into the deepening hole.

Chad ought not to have brought the other along, he might catch a chill, it could turn to pneumonia. Or collapse with a heart attack. Kroll was merciless towards those who offended him.

'Take a breather, Larry.' Chad was up to his thighs now. 'There's only room for me to work now else we'll get in each other's way.'

'Please your flamin' self, then!' Larry stood back, he would never admit that he was tiring. 'I worked for Victor's dad during the war, skinflint he was, too. I dug all them graves over there, from the yew tree right down to the path.' He pointed behind him. 'Every one of 'em on me flippin' own. A pound a grave, he paid me, wouldn't go to any more.'

'Slave labour,' Chad grunted as he lifted out another clod of mud.

'I remember the winter of 1947,' Larry went on, 'the snow was the deepest I ever know'd it, came on January twenty-seventh and lasted right through till March tenth. And just when it started to thaw, another blizzard came and filled it all in again. We 'ad corpses queuing up to be buried that winter!' He cackled throatily. 'Dug all the graves on my own that Spring but I never thought I'd see the day when I'd be diggin' one up again!'

Chad's shovel thudded on something that sounded hollow. 'I think we're almost there, Larry.'

'We should've brought ropes to haul the coffin up.'

'We won't need to, all I want is a look.'

'To say hallo like?'

'You've got it.' Chad shivered, felt his sweat chill.

He began scraping the soil off a flat, smooth surface. 'Pass me the torch, Larry.'

Chad directed the beam downwards, breathed a sigh of relief as its light revealed brass handles and screws still firmly embedded in the woodwork. 'Well, he hasn't got out, or, if he has, he's screwed his coffin up before he left!' It was meant to be a joke but it sounded decidedly unfunny in the silence of a moonlit graveyard.

'Them vampire creatures used to close theirs up,' Larry said sounding nervous, 'then go back to 'em at dawn. Like beds. I remember seein' a film about 'em once, in the days when we had a cinema in town. It's gone now.'

Thanks a bundle and fuck you, Larry. 'Throw the screw-driver down, please.'

It thudded on to the coffin, Chad picked it up with shaking fingers. Maybe there wasn't really any need to look, nobody had got out of there. He took a deep breath, it was tonight or never, there wouldn't be a second chance. Lindy had gone to stay with her parents in Llanidloes, she hadn't seen them since before the snow came.

'Promise me you won't get up to anything whilst I'm gone, Chad.' She had pleaded with him, watched him suspiciously.

'What is there to get up to? Kroll's gone. For ever.'

'I . . . I kinda feel that . . . that he's still around, you can't see him but he's watching you all the time.' She was spooked like the rest of the townspeople. 'They didn't find any of his . . . *remains* in the ashes of his house.' Lindy had clung to him, trembled.

'Look, love, there's nothing left for me to investigate, it's all over. The paper didn't get a story, they never will now.'

'All the same, promise me that you won't go poking around, looking for trouble.'

'All right, I promise.'

That promise was already broken. Opening up the coffin made no difference from now on.

The screws were tight, Chad had to exert force, heard a cracking of wood as the first one loosened.

'Screwed the bugger in tight, 'asn't he?' Larry peered over the edge, a silhouette against the starry sky. 'Afraid 'e might get out, maybe.'

Shut up, Larry, for Christ's sake!

The second screw was seated even more firmly. Chad gouged for it, prised it until it came free amidst a cluster of splinters.

God, it stank down here! The stench seared his throat, had him retching. It was like something rotten. Which was true, Edward Kroll decomposed in his coffin, the empty screw holes had released the smell.

Three down, one to go.

'Doin' OK?' Larry sounded impatient, he was probably freezing.

Go, home, Larry, sit by the fire. No, don't go and leave me alone. 'Almost there.'

'We gotta fill it all in again, don't forget.'

'I hadn't forgotten.'

The fourth screw was even more stubborn than the rest, resisted his efforts. *You've no business looking in here, Chad. Go now, whilst there's still time.*

I want a good look at you, Edward Kroll. I'll never rest easy until I see for myself that you're really dead.

'Takin' your time, ain't you?'

Chad did not answer. The groove in the screw head had twisted, the screwdriver kept slipping out of it. He stabbed at the woodwork, he'd have to dig this one right out by the look of it.

'Havin' trouble?'

'Just a . . . little.' The wood split but the screw did not move.

'Victor's a good craftsman, give 'im 'is due. Once 'e's screwed a stiff down, 'e don't mean nobody goin' lookin' at it.'

'I believe you, Larry.'

The lid cracked, split across its entire width.

'Sounds 'opeful.'

The full force of that vile stench came up at Chad, had him recoiling, turning his head away. *Go on, lift the lid, take a looksee.*

You have been warned.

'That it?'

Chad gave way to a spasm of coughing.

'What're you waitin' for?'

Chad groped for the edge of the lid with soil encrusted, trembling fingers. He found a hold, braced himself. There was no room to manoeuvre down here, the torch shook in his free hand, its beam wavered and dimmed a little. As if it was scared and shaking, too.

The smell seemed different suddenly, it took him a few seconds to identify it. A charred stench like a fire that had burned and consumed, gone cold.

It was just his imagination.

'Smells like sommat's been burned down there.'

The coffin lid came up easily, would have thrown Chad off balance if he had not been within the confines of the grave. His earthy fingers lost their hold and it fell back with a soft thud.

Because he was not meant to see inside.

Fuck you! He grasped it again, made sure that he had a firmer grip this time. It seemed heavier than before, creaked as it was uplifted. He leaned it upright against the earthen wall; a trickle of soil and small stones pattered on to something soft.

'Shine the light, let's 'ave a look at the blighter, then.' Larry was leaning right over the graveside in his morbid curiosity.

Chad forced himself to look, knew that he was shying away from whatever lay in the coffin. Relief came first because the corpse was there, its absence would have been too much for his logic, his sanity, to accept. Then he was recoiling in revulsion from that which the fading circle of torchlight revealed.

'It's *him* no mistake about that.' Maybe Larry's eyesight was failing after nine decades, or it was the dim light that spared him the awful details.

Kroll had shrunken in death, or it might have been that Chad had never before seen him without the oversize topcoat that hid the true extent of his emaciation. The shroud was crumpled, like bedsheets tossed to one side in the heat of a fever. He was grotesque in his smallness, obscene in death. Or was it sleep? The eyes were open, stared angrily as if they saw and were aware of this intrusion of the grave.

The nostrils were clogged with solidified mucus, even in life it would have been impossible to breathe through them; the mouth was half-open, the lips preparing to speak, reviling a grave robber. Chad instinctively cupped his hands over his ears in case he heard.

Wasted in life but not decomposing in death: possibly the frozen ground had preserved the sparse flesh until now; it was the flesh that was the most awful feature of all.

It was stretched over the bones as taut as ever, but it was no longer translucent. Instead, it was grimed and smoke-blackened, a roast that had been forgotten in an oven: charred to a crisp but otherwise unchanged.

'Finished?' If Larry had noticed the change in Kroll's skin texture then he maybe thought that the corpse was bathed in dark grave shadows.

Chad let the lid fall shut, more stones and earth spilled down from the vibration like passing mourners had tossed them.

Fill in the grave, bury the cadaver so that never again shall human eyes look upon it.

Chad and Larry shovelled furiously, did not pause in their efforts until all that remained of their night's work was an oblong mound of fresh earth. Nobody would ever know that it had been disturbed except he who lay below.

Chad prayed that Edward Kroll would remain there. For ever.

Twenty-Three

'Your name, sir?'

The grey-suited clerk did not even glance up from behind his heavy-lensed spectacles. He was not interested in faces or appearances, all that mattered in his business was names. Faces were of no consequence; you could not computerize features.

'Kroll. Spelled K . . . R . . . O . . . L . . . L. E for Edward.'

'Thank you, sir. And you wish to trace your descendants?' A bored question, almost everybody who came into the General Register Office was searching for their roots. He didn't bother to stifle his yawn.

'That is correct.'

'Their full names, place of birth, date of death. If known.'

The other hesitated, appeared to be embarrassed for a moment. 'I had an uncle. Also called Edward. I'm not sure of the others, even if there are any. It's an unusual name. Our family history was destroyed in a fire recently.'

The clerk's features remained expressionless. 'As you say, sir, an unusual name. Fortunately. I'll run it up on the microfiche, see what comes up. If you'd care to take a seat, sir, the process will take several minutes.'

'Thank you.'

Chad sat down. So far, so good. He was tense but in a different way from how he'd been that night, a few months ago, when he and Larry had dug up Kroll's grave. Now, as then, you didn't know what you might find. If anything.

Maybe this facade, this thinly veiled impersonation, wasn't necessary. Anybody was entitled to ask to see any files, but it had seemed more appropriate if you were family. A sudden impulse that now made him feel slightly foolish.

It was a long shot, the last one left; he'd play it. If nothing came of it, he'd try to forget it. If anybody could ever forget Edward Kroll and his reign of terror that had ended in an inferno one wintry night.

If it had ended.

The General Register Office was awesome in its uniformity. Like the counter clerk. So impersonal, there was nothing that would stick in your memory, nothing that you would remember yet you found yourself in dread of officialdom. Like a tourist exploring a cathedral. But cathedrals had architecture to interest even the godless.

Things were changing back in Knighton, Chad reflected. The Morgans had sold the Grillhouse, bought another eating establishment in Newtown; some people from away had purchased the Grillhouse, it was rumoured that they intended to serve French cuisine. They'd probably be bankrupt within a year. Betty Wilkins's house had been sold to a local tradesman; now it was a craft shop.

Phil Morris had been promoted to sergeant and had moved to Llandrindod Wells. He deserved it. Ken Davison was due to retire at the end of the summer.

Kroll's house was untouched, a gutted ruin. It was still not known who the insurers were, if any. Until they were located, nobody would pay for its rebuilding. It would remain a scar upon the town, a detriment to tourism.

Just as if it was waiting for him to return.

If the police had attempted to track down Kroll's past then their findings had not been made public. He had committed no crime, he was merely missing. They probably had not found out anything, anyway. A series of 'accidental' deaths, however bizarre, did not warrant an investigation. Was it an offence for one to return from the grave to resume life? Certainly not when neither medical records nor a certificate of death could be produced. The laws of the land did not cater for impossibilities, factors that defied the cycle of life.

Chad had to know the answers for his own peace of mind.

'Mr Kroll, sir.'

Chad started out of his reverie, the clerk was seated back at his desk, held up a small white card.

'Oh, yes.' Chad's stomach knotted, the moment of truth was a terrifying prospect.

'Please go through to the public search room.' A finger pointed in the direction of a doorway at the far end. 'Hand this to the search clerk and he will provide you with the information you require.'

Chad was shaking, he fought off an impulse to turn round and walk right back out into the street. Some things in life, and death, were better not known.

He glanced at the ballpoint scrawl on the card: Kroll, Ambrose, No: 640551.

The search clerk might have been a brother to the one in reception, such was the similarity amongst this faceless army of bureaucrats. Even their mannerisms were identical.

'Please take a seat, sir.'

Waiting again. This room was much smaller than the outer one, a semi-circular desk segregated officialdom from the public and their time-consuming enquiries.

'Please take a seat, sir.'

There was a woman seated nearby. She wore a black two-piece that matched her raven hair. She did not look up. Chad thought that she was grieving.

It was like sitting in a doctor's surgery, embarrassment because others were wondering why you were here; fear because of what the diagnosis might reveal.

'Thank you, Mrs Hartford.'

The woman rose unsteadily to her feet, took a sheet of paper which the clerk handed to her. She made no attempt to open it up. Clutching it in her hand, she walked straight out of the door, did not look back. Chad knew that he would never see her again.

'I won't keep you a moment, sir.'

The moment stretched to quarter of an hour, then the clerk returned; an identical ritual followed with another sheet of folded photocopy.

'Thank you.' Chad went back to his seat, he did not trust his legs to walk him all the way back to the underground station.

He winced when the paper rustled as he smoothed it out,

experienced guilt in the same way as he'd done as a boy in church when his candy papers distracted a praying congregation. The clerk didn't look up, he was hunched over a keyboard, tapping with two fingers.

Chad's vision blurred for a moment, the printed words became illegible, the paper shook so that he couldn't have read them, anyway. Then everything cleared and the photocopy stopped shaking.

Kroll. Ambrose.

Just a namesake, probably.

Date of birth: 22nd February, 1923.

In all likelihood this guy was no relation at all.

Place of birth: Knighton, Radnorshire.

Jesus Almighty! Chad went icy cold, the paper started rustling and shaking again so that he could no longer read it.

OK, he'd go along with the brother angle, it fitted George Edmonds' theory that Edward Kroll died and was buried, and some weeks later an identical twin had turned up in town, carried on where Edward had left off; that there *had* been a number of accidental deaths, pure coincidences. That made it real easy, locked the bogeyman back in the cupboard and everybody could sleep easy again. Documents did get lost, no matter how careful you were.

The fire? Ambrose had not been home at the time so his ashes were not found in the debris. He'd maybe gone on a cruise or a sunshine holiday for the winter months.

Which meant that he'd be back.

Chad's spine prickled. But there was nothing to worry about.

Except that Edward Kroll was fire-blackened in his grave. And, officially, he had not existed, neither in life nor death.

Another train of thought shunted out of the sidings of Chad's mind. Find Ambrose Kroll and the whole mystery would be solved; George Edmonds wanted to talk to him about Edward's probate. Look for Ambrose, not Edward. The bogeyman would be vanquished for ever, it had all been a big mistake, exaggerated out of all proportion by coincidences and rumours spread by a close-knit community that lived behind locked doors and closed curtains.

Chad looked back down at the sheet of photocopy and that was when his hopes disintegrated in one brain-shattering explosion.

He felt dizzy, thought he might faint. Gut-wrenching nausea had bile scorching his throat, he might throw up.

'Are you all right, Mr Kroll?'

The clerk was human, after all.

Kroll, Edward. Kroll, Ambrose. Whichever, it mattered not.

Date of death . . .

Chad felt his fingers crumpling the photostat, compressing it into a ball, compacting it. Destroying it because it was irrelevant. The information on it was of no further use to himself nor anybody else, never had been.

Because Ambrose Kroll had died ten years ago.

Twenty-Four

The boy moved swiftly along the deserted street; darting, furtive movements, stopping to listen every few metres. He made no sound as he walked.

The ruined house was silhouetted gauntly against the starry sky, a warm breeze moaned through the gutted windows as if the place breathed deeply in slumber.

The figure dropped into a crouch as it approached the blackened doorway, holding back as though afraid, debating whether or not to flee before he was discovered. Again he checked that there was nobody in sight.

He stood peering in through the doorway but it was impossible to see in the darkness. He backed away, afraid to enter.

His head was uplifted but his features remained in shadow. He sniffed the air like a creature of the wild that was afraid lest some beast of prey waited in ambush.

A sudden gust of wind buffeted the ruin, moaned through the desolation, a noise like a cry of pain and anguish from a demented soul in eternal damnation.

The boy turned and fled, sped soundlessly back whence he had come. Whatever he had sensed or heard, he would not be returning.

The wind dropped and all was silent again within the fire ravaged house.